Victorious

AN ARMY AWAKENS

VICTORIA BOYSON

VICTORIOUS: AN ARMY AWAKENS

Victoria Boyson Ministries

www.victoriaboyson.com

victoria@boyson.org

Victorious

AN ARMY AWAKENS

CONTENTS

DEDICATION

This book is dedicated to all those who are lost and without a true understanding of their heavenly Father, Who loves them and Who sent His only Son, Jesus, to die as a sacrifice to deliver them of their sins and give them lives of real freedom and abounding joy!

Father, I ask you to use this book to awaken your church and redeem those who need you so desperately. Help them to know you.

Acknowledgements

Thank you to those who helped me bring this last book of the series to life. Your help and prayer were immeasurable. I know it would not have happened without you.

Bless you Cassandra Boyson, Steve Boyson and Derene Shultz.

Introduction

Dear Friends,

THE LORD IS as creative in communicating His truths to us as He is in designing His creation. I believe the visions and dreams He gives us are a lot like the parables He gave in the Bible. Many people, including myself, learn His truth best from parables and visions that help clarify the Word of God.

This book, *Victorious,* is the last in a series, preceded by *Awakening* and *Revolution.* All came to me through visions the Lord gave me over several years, which I call *The Deep Sleep trilogy.* As God called me to write down the visions He gave me, it felt very much like being called to a visionary journey. I've tried to make it as descriptive as I saw it, so you would feel as though you were right there with Beloved, our heroine. I wanted to be faithful to the words He gave and the imagery He showed me so I could, without reservation, assure you it was from Him to you.

Over thirty years ago, my mother went to her true home in heaven's realm. Since that time, my awareness of that realm has been more than awakened, and sometimes I feel as much a part of it as the earth. One of my favorite Scriptures is Colossians 3:1-3, "If then you were raised with Christ, seek those things which are above, where Christ is, sitting at the right hand of God. Set your mind on things above, not on things on the earth. For you died, and your life is hidden with Christ in God." (KJV, emphasis mine).

In this life, I've found true reality only as I've experienced this life "hidden with Christ," living not for a temporal purpose but for the eternal goals of God's heavenly kingdom. His kingdom is as real as the world we live in and as we seek to know Him better, we will learn of His kingdom, becoming stewards of the kingdom of heaven on earth.

In these moments, I feel the great heavenly company of witnesses urging me to remain wide awake – faithful to my focused earthly purpose and keeping watchful for the tricks that can dull the senses in this world. I feel shaken by the true reality of heaven, as if something of eternal importance is taking place, and the urgency is alarming.

Our world is under the effects of a supernatural war, in which the kingdom of darkness is trying with all its strength to convince the world the only reality is this *world's system.* Successfully, they've locked away the minds of generations into a way of thinking, excluding an understanding of their heavenly home, and their loving heavenly Father. We've been told that most of this world is secular with only a small portion of it belonging to God. That is a lie. God created this world and every good thing. Satan can only copy the good creations of our God. He's led key world leaders to believe they could actually take over this world for Satan, but that is also a lie.

When this series of books, *Awakening, Revolution* and lastly, *Victorious,* came to me I thought it would be a fun little journey with God. Yet, after finishing *Revolution* and beginning on *Victorious,* I under-went three years of unrelenting attack from the enemy. During that time, I saw the underbelly of the enemy and learned much. It was horrible, but it was only when I realized it was this book they were trying to stop that everything became clear. In trying to stop it, they gave away many secrets that would empower those who read it. No one really knows what the future holds, but as the Holy Spirit downloaded these visions to me, I was seeing a reality in it, both of devilish evil, and a victorious reality unveiled.

Make no mistake about it, God will awaken us to His reality, but how He does it depends on each one of us. Whether easy or difficult, early or late, God will make us Victorious if we let Him.

— Victoria

THE FALSE BRIDE

MAKING HER WAY through the dense, dark forest, Beloved was a determined traveler. She was confident Holy Spirit was leading her and His heart speaking to her was earnest in her prospective journey. The night was permeated with a damp coldness that made her spirit shiver, but she longed to give an answer to the pervasive questions of her heart. Although this forest had terrified her in the past, with unwavering bravery, she continued to plunge through the trees that were laden with sorcerous power determined to hinder her progress.

As she traveled, she remembered all she had endured since her awakening from the deep sleep. Memories flooded her mind of the lonely separation from the prophetic host she loved so much, and the painful recollection of her visit to the river of shame where millions were held captive by deception, awaiting their unfortunate end. She knew no matter what she'd endured, her mission had not changed. Indeed, Lord Jesus had commissioned her and the host to awaken the sleeping masses, who were to become His last-days army. Truly, without them she would not stand a hope of saving anyone from the grip of the river's strong current.

On and through she proceeded, pressing through heavy branches, searching for a clearing in the dense woods. She could see very little at this point and in the dark all things attempted to undermine her courage, to distract and convince her of the hopelessness of her journey. Climbing over large downed trees and rocks that seemed determined to hinder her progress, only obedience could persuade her to seek out this place on her own, for the path was heavy with dark spirits and demonic oppression.

Beloved had been terrified of this forest when Jesus had taken her to the river of shame. However, through the attacks launched against her, fear concerning it could no longer hold her. Yet, she knew instinctively that the journey would be one of the greatest tests of her life. Indeed, after what seemed like an eternity of desperate struggle through the forest, she sensed a break in the trees ahead. She could hear what she thought was the rippling of water running up a river's banks. The air smelled old, dank and made her shudder as if laden with death.

Slowing as she neared the end of the woods, she tarried to survey the scene. It was then she spotted the outline of a tall, slender woman standing in the light of the full moon, while the thick, hovering trees clung to the night like a dark oppressive shadow.

As she approached the scene, she noticed the woman was dressed as a bride. Beloved could only see the outline of a gown and veil lit up by the faint light breaking upon her while the figure stared out aimlessly over the intense dark water.

Beloved wondered why a bride would be there. Was she searching the water in anticipation of someone?

Suddenly, as Beloved came up from behind her, the bride turned abruptly to face her as if she had been expecting her.

Jumping back at the sight of her, Beloved jolted with fright at the woman's sudden advance. Her concentrated gaze filled her with uneasiness, while the shadows of the forest hid the bride's face from view.

Curiosity kept Beloved in her place as much as the comfort she felt from her Holy Guide, who spoke to her heart. His words kept her calm as she peered back, trying desperately to see the woman clearly in the dim moonlight.

As the dark clouds of the night drifted past the moon, its light shone brighter for a moment, revealing the woman's face. Beloved's piercing gasp of horror stabbed like a knife into the stillness of the night.

Overwhelmed with dread, her feet seemed nailed to the ground while her eyes could not leave the face before her.

The woman was indeed a bride, but her countenance was not beautiful nor was it a normal human face. No, the bride wore two faces, both of equal emptiness. Grotesquely, she stared at Beloved through her vacant dark eyes. Her black hair shone with blue tints as the moonlight revealed its dirty, stringy tresses that seemed alive with hidden creatures concealed within its unkempt coiffures.

Torn and disheveled, her gown was as distorted as her facial expression. Although resembling bridal attire, it was blackened into a bedraggled, straggly state. She couldn't be certain whether she should pity the woman or defend herself against her.

Beloved stood frozen in confused fear by the woman's appearance. Suddenly, the bride opened both her mouths to speak. Her voice was like a hundred voices speaking all at once, reverberating through a thousand cold, hallow caverns, and it settled over her like a blanket of oppressive fear.

"Greetings, Beloved. I'm so glad yoooou havve cooome heree. I have beeeeen foooollowing youu. How special you areee! So verrrry special. You have vaaaluable insight, Beloved. Vaaaluable. You are sooooooo giiiifted. So gifffted." She hissed as she attempted to flatter her, but her flattery unsettled Beloved and the woman was visibly displeased at not receiving the appreciative response she'd expected. As vexation swept over her faces, her eyes flashed with an inner rage.

In an attempt at stifling her anger, the woman continued. *"You have poteeeeential, Beloved,"* she hissed with pretended discernment while vainly masking condescending disdain. As she tried to gain the upper hand, she leaned into Beloved and said, "*I would like to help you, sweeeetie. I could realllly help you, Beloved. Do you seeee all I have created heere?*" She motioned with her hands toward the expanse of the thick, black lake that was filled with those who'd chosen a life of idolatry and witchcraft. It was clear those within were proud to be there. Basking in their assumed power, they had no idea they were held captive.

The woman waited for her reaction, almost daring her to show her true emotions so she could explode her wrath, but Beloved managed to disguise her disapproval of the murky abyss.

Attempting to bait Beloved, she switched from condescension to passive aggression. "*I've been watching you, young woman, and I know aaaalll about you. You have such a cute, little mission; it's just darling. I will praaaaay for you, Beloved.*"

Beloved's eyebrows shot up in response to her blatant rudeness and threat of "prayer," which encouraged the woman to continue. With a widening smirk, she added, "*I can be of greeaatt assistance to you, my sweeetie,*" lips dripping with lordliness. "*I know sooooo many people... I have soooooo many friends.... All those who matter follow me. I've worked with..."* as she continued, Beloved's mind began to wander.

She sensed in her spirit a figure approaching them from somewhere behind her. It was just entering the dark woods. Beloved felt certain it was someone sent by the Father to help her face this foe.

"...just to name a few!"

Her attention snapped back.

"Who do yoooou know, Beloved?"

Beloved couldn't answer. Her mind froze with the question that felt more like an accusation.

"Of course, I know you have such a smaaaall host of prophetic friends, but you have been drudging after Jehovah. What has He dooone for you? He's forgotten all about yooou. Do you really think He meant to heeelp you, Beloved. He doesn't even know you are aliiive. If you will put yourself in myyyy hands, I can make you BIGGG! I know eeeeeveryone who maaatters, I will promoote you. You are sooo small, just a baaaaby, because you've been laaazy and you don't know the right peeeople. You are being waaasted. You're gifts are so precccccious, Beloved. I can heeelp you use your giiiiifftts."

Beloved could bare no more. Her heart and mind were flooded with a hazy fog that made her hope sink. She wrestled with reality. To hear her mission - which she viewed as more of a journey of love with her heavenly Father - talked about in such a shallow manner, unsettled her. She deeply felt the impact of the accusations against the Father. Beloved began to feel all wrong in herself.

Sensing Beloved's weakness, the creature grew more emboldened with her. *"I was told allll about you, Beloved. You cause trouble wheeerever you go. You are a baaaad seed. They said you were neeegative, but I stuck up for you. I told them that you were only negative because you didn't praaay enough, like I do. What do you say to that, Beloooovveed?"* She smiled broadly in both faces as she wove her words around every accusation with intention to embed each one deep into Beloved's heart.

Beloved, close to tears, pleaded with her, *"What do you want from me?"*

"What do III waaant from youuu…?" She threw her head back and laughed, shaking the trees all around them. *"Nothing but your soul, dear one."* She continued looking right through Beloved, searing her mind with her round black eyes. *"That's*

all! I want you to boooow to me and worship me. There is sooo much God has kept from you. Heee didn't want you to know the truth about meee. He knows I haaave the power to answer your heart'sss desires. I have what you neeeed! Live while you are young, giiirl. Did God reeeaaally say there would be a judgment daaay? Did He saaay you can only seerve Him? What is He afraaaid of? If you don't worship meee, you will neveer experience the depths of truuuuth I alone possess. You will neeever know trueee enlightenment."

Her mouth stopped moving now. Held stationary, it began to drool as her vicious voices continued to speak. *"You will suffer with the reeest of the looow-life on Earth, while weee attain hiiigher levels of spiritual nothingnesssss. You won't need to ssserve God, Beloved. You can becoooome God. All I want is your soul. And I will give you the wooorld..."* she continued as the lake behind her grew even darker.

Coming alive, it whispered with activity. Something was stirring within it. Then, like a beast awaiting its prey, what had seemed like vague, dull malevolence in the water was suddenly awakening with unprovoked licentious delight.

The river was teeming with evil creations of the dark bride's wantonness, witchcraft and idolatry of every kind. All who had given her their worship were held captive. Even those who'd wanted her power gave over every accursed chain of their life's meaning to her. And her dark lake was filled with her worshipers.

A dark, penetrating shadow fell across the woman's face that spread into a lurid grin. Her attempted perversion of God's motives had done the trick and all the old demons that plagued Beloved were finding their familiar home in her thoughts. As she accepted the well rehearsed lies, the atmosphere around her grew even more sinister and vicious.

Desperately seeking heavenly Father's wisdom, Beloved felt nothing in her spirit but blank emptiness. *"Father!"* she whispered. *"Help me, Father!"*

Falling back toward the dark forest and hitting the hardened black dirt, Beloved's consciousness searched for her boundaries. Needing something to give her a sense of who she was, the battles of her past deluged her mind. Like a torrent, the flood of accusations worked to convince her she was bad, abased and would be damned. Feeling unworthy of mercy, self-hatred and shame crept in all around, caressing her shoulders like an old friend. She felt herself losing control.

Horrified, Beloved searched for wisdom, but her mind was being lulled down into the easy path of least resistance. The darkened forest behind her fluttered with excitement, matching the degeneracy and evil of the lake. Struggling on the ground in emotional agony, all Beloved could do was watch as this evil woman stood over her, waiting to deal the final blow.

Studying her with donnish delight, the evil bride watched as hopelessness grabbed on to Beloved's mind. Hitting at her with the old familiar lies, demons poured over her like a starving mob. Now with rapt viciousness, they scrambled to regain their possession once again, eager to recover their lost territory. She was a prize!

All the lake's creatures, especially the dark bride, knew what Beloved really meant to the kingdom of the Creator. She felt proud to have coerced the mind of the Father's Beloved. So, with the return of their bounty, they attacked with unparalleled ferocity. Jealous hatred disguised as pious nobleness fueled their war against her, impatient to enslave her mind again.

"There's something really wrooong with you," the woman jabbed with a voice dripping with disdain. *"No one will ever love you. No one has ever wanted you. It's the way you act. You need to fixxxxxx yourself. You are pointless. What use are you? You are too weak; you need to be more powerful. You are too merciful. You are too negative, too sensitive, too positive."* The words were all too familiar to her, and in the woman, Beloved saw all the faces of those who'd been used to accuse her in her past. And they sang out like a chorus of destructive wolves.

As long, dark tentacles began to unfurl themselves from underneath the counterfeit bride's gown, the black lake, too, joined the demons in their song as if to distract Beloved with an evil dirge of demonic declarations. Orchestrated by the evil creature, the atmosphere was filled with their sinister heinous music, while her tentacles crept subtly toward her prey.

Enjoying their triumph over her, the creatures of the dark lake sang out with evil glee, *"There muuust be something wrooong with you!"* While the phony bride felt heinous enjoyment that nearly made her drunk with sadism, reveling in the pain she'd caused Beloved.

Lying with her face in the dirt, Beloved wanted to give up and die. But something in her began to feel a semblance of strength, so, looking to the Father, she let the death-filled words being sung over her penetrate her mind. They washed over her and she started thanking God for every horrendous word and accusation thrown against her. For, they were causing the death of all that needed to die in her, all the things in her heart that clung to the approval of others. The wanting desperately to be understood had made her weak and vulnerable to their abuse. She let it consume her until there was nothing left in her that cared about their opinions and accusations, until there was nothing left but the righteousness of Christ - which was one immovable reality they could not take away. *Indeed, I am nothing, but, in Him, I am everything He is!* she reasoned in her mind.

As she lay, she felt the ease of pain leaving her soul and it made her heart laughed - a little a first, and then more. She knew she was dead to them and Holy Spirit's strength was rising in her...

"I don't care," she whispered to herself as she lay facing the dirt. She was conscious of the sudden quiver of fear that shot through her accusers as her

whispered words were felt in the spirit-realm. But she wasn't saying it for their benefit; it just felt good to say the words. She was saying it for her own heart, so she said it again, "*I don't care.*" Again and again, she proclaimed the words. It made her happy to say them, because she truly meant them.

She felt freedom and delighted in it as she spoke the words over and over to herself. She ministered to herself as she lay in the dirt. Eyes closed, she felt her heart opening to Holy Spirit's growing power in her as she proclaimed the truth.

Suddenly, she saw in the spirit a giant hand reach out for her. A beautiful hand Beloved knew she could trust came right to her face. She could see it in detail and knew instantly it was the hand of Lord Jesus, her Rescuer. She reached up and grabbed it with both her hands and embraced it with a kiss. He then brought her up into His lap and made her feel like a little girl again, safe and protected. Oh, how He loved her.

All of a sudden, she was taken up into a Mighty Current of Wind. Instantly propelled straight up into the sky, she burst out of the earth's atmosphere. Above the cosmos of the planet, she hovered in the midst of open space. Held by the hand of the Lord in the moonlight, caliginous except for the moon and the thousands of stars gleaming down on her in brilliant splendor. Breathtaking stillness engaged her senses like a gentle breeze, she felt free from the fears of the earth and was entirely herself as Father had designed her.

"I'm not afraid of the dark anymore, Jesus," she spoke into the atmosphere of space.

Suddenly, shafts of light filled with dancing sparkles shot up from the earth and encircled her as if it were dressing her in a gown of translucent, illuminated streams of Shekinah Glory. Around and around, they circled her until she was covered in streams of light of various hues. Lastly, it surrounded her head, crowning Beloved with a garland of brilliance. Cocooned by the light, she felt embraced and loved. She knew then the light was Holy Spirit as He restored her soul, reclaiming her from the attacks she'd endured.

Feeling strength like she'd never known cascading through the rawness of her soul, she felt like a baby again held in the arms of the Great Comforter. Restored, they descended slowly back to Earth, both enjoying the moment.

As Her Precious Friend and Comforter returned her to the earth, Beloved awakened to find herself in the same place, but she was not the same person and her accusers knew it.

2

THE BATTLE OF
TWO BRIDES

WITH THE POWERFUL transformation of her heart, Beloved felt a tremendous change in the atmosphere. As her eyes glanced questioningly around her, she wondered if her heart alone had changed or if something more had transpired.

Looking around, she found the same murky, black lake, and the two-faced woman in dark, dingy veil and gown, damp dirt and wide-sweeping dark woods that seemed to frame her. It seemed nothing had changed and yet, she was certain it had.

The woman seemed older now and much less threatening. Beloved felt more pity for her than fear. The lines in her face made her appear ancient and tired. Her expression looked strange, with a scowl directed at her, but Beloved felt only sorrow for her and did not internalize her obvious disapproval.

An armed resolve radiated from the scornful woman that manifested as disdainful contempt. Yet, she knew Beloved's heart had changed.

The false bride's resolve, however, made her tremendously petulant, like a powder keg ready to explode. Seething as she watched Beloved, the woman studied her for any possible avenues of attack. While probing her for signs of weakness, she'd become completely unaware of her own very evident failing. The woman was completely convinced of her own power and was obviously enamored with it. While convinced she was impervious to attack, she continued her guise.

Beloved barely even noticed that, while she was seated with her back to the woods, a beautiful woman had walked quietly through the dark forest and sat down next to her. When she realized she was no longer alone in this difficult place, she was completely overwhelmed by this new woman's appearance.

Astonished, Beloved lit up when she realized the woman was another bride!

She wore a simple, long, white gown, with glorious long sheer sleeves, pearl buttons and yards and yards of white chiffon fabric that gleamed in response to the dark place. Certainly, she was the complete antithesis of the first bride. Sitting next to Beloved upon the dirty, dank ground like a diamond sitting upon a crown, she radiated a peace that pervaded the atmosphere and made her resplendent in appearance.

As Beloved turned toward her with eyes of wonder, the bride smiled and said cheerfully, *"Hello."*

This bride embodied incredible purity and joy. Beloved reasoned she'd never in her life seen such joy before!

She knew instinctively this beautiful woman was the true bride of Christ Jesus, yet, she looked so unlike what Beloved had expected. Indeed, by contrast to her thinking, this bride seemed more like a girl than a woman. She was delightfully full of mirth and light and smiled with such animated merriment it left Beloved to marvel in admiration.

What an unassuming figure! Beloved thought to herself.

She sat alongside Beloved with gleeful interest in the dark, forlorn woman that glared down at them both. In amazed response, it seemed that all activity in the dark forest stood still for a moment, as if frozen in time.

Beloved, too, in astonished amazement, felt tongue-tied and simply watched the scene transform. Those who'd so recently held her in a life and death struggle made a sudden twist in their temperaments. The dark waters seemed to cool in their fierce activity as though it were bolted up by a gale of wind. And just as surely, the ominous forest arrested its attention as if it were grabbed by an unseen force overhead. All but the dark bride were frozen in a stupor, and even Beloved could not help but hesitate in her response to the beautifully captivating woman.

With artless pride, Beloved happily sat near the bride, who presently held the scene in her grasp. Carefree, and as easy as a bird in a tree, she was unmoved. Turning her bright eyes on Beloved's amazed face, she reached out her arms. Pulling Beloved close to her, she offered a disarming smile. As though they'd known each other their whole lives, they were washed in familiar friendship. Her confidence increased in this uneasy place, with the true bride's acceptance.

Studying the dark bride again, Beloved viewed her through eyes bathed in truth. She knew then what strength she'd held inside herself all along. Indeed, it was the pitifully dark and brutal figure before her who was the weak one and not herself.

It was she, and not Beloved at all, who was the accused and condemned, holding in her all the misery she'd tried to unleash on Beloved. She could no longer hide the twisted reasoning of her manipulated countenance.

Realizing Beloved now beheld her only as a figure to be pitied, the hideous creature rose in black rage seething visible hostility.

"NOOOOOOO!!!!" the evil woman screamed into the atmosphere, shaking everything in the dark place.

Everything within the woman seemed to lose control and exploded in Beloved's direction. Lunging at her, the false bride flew at her throat, but was stopped suddenly by a simple shining small arm. With stalwart limb raised, the young bride stopped her and needed only to remind the old woman that she was there.

Engulfing the attention of the atmosphere, the old woman boiled with rage as she obediently returned to her place, arrested by the invisible grasp of the young bride. Attempting to regain the fearful control of Beloved's heart, her rage struck out of her like lightning in her hard-earned, dark kingdom.

Responding to her rage, those in the water's grasp rose up. With intense offense and hostility, each one raged at Beloved and released stored up animosity toward her. Yet, the atmosphere had changed, filled with an intensity that Beloved did not understand. She felt quite strongly that all that had occurred in her life had been leading up to this moment and everyone there understood that clearly but her.

Jumping to attention, the young bride moved swiftly toward the two-faced hag, who'd fought hard to usurp the true bride's role. As she moved in between Beloved and the woman, the forest and the dark lake came alive and filled the atmosphere with sharp shrills and shrieks of chaos and fear. Propelling up in the water as if to attract attention, faces fought recklessly, striving to rise higher than the others around them. Even the trees tried desperately to move and affect an element of fear on the two of them.

Horrific as they were in their desperacy, the young bride was unmoved by them. She'd encountered them before and understood their game. It mattered less to her than as if they were completely invisible. All they did only strengthened her as she stood resilient against their attempts to intimidate.

This glorious bride was impervious to fear!

As the bride's fearlessness became apparent to all present, her countenance radiated an intense golden glow of an unearthly Presence. As the Presence reached her, the usurper was consumed in violent, fearful hatred. Exploding with rage, she reached for the neck of the beautiful bride. Held back by the Presence, she continued to strike at her with electrified bolts of hatred that shot out from her hands. Her eyes revealed the source of her power, enveloped by a light-blue fire that radiated out of her like talons as she tried desperately to attack the young woman.

"Your time of deception is coming to an end and you know it," the true bride struck at her with truth. *"You've tried to substitute your Babylonian games for the relationship God wants to have with His children. You are being exposed as a fake and a liar! For years, you've raised up your false gods as*

though they were the One True God and drawn the masses to you, yet you still haven't been able to snuff out my Light! You had all the advantage, nonetheless you've failed. Now, it's my turn to show you the power of the Almighty God!"

As Beloved watched the intense struggle of the counterfeit bride, she realized the surpassing power the true bride possessed. As impressive as it was to Beloved, its discovery enraged the false bride even more. She knew the Presence all too well and could hide no longer. She became entirely possessed of something completely unearthly and monstrous, full of an overwhelming hatred that made Beloved shudder as she watched it possess her.

"If you think I will just back away after all I've invested, you will be disappointed," the false bride answered back. *"I've already defamed your Scriptures and sown seeds of deception into your churches. My best warriors fill your sanctuaries, disguised as deep spiritual thinkers. And I promise I will draw the weak believers away from you with my idolatrous witchcraft, because so many of His children love my magic. It makes them feel so powerful."* She smirked through snarling lips. *"I will take as many as I can down with me! They will believe me, because I have what they think deep*

truth looks like and they're easily fooled. In me, they believe they've found their Shangri-la." She threw back her head and nearly howled in laughter while the black lake rejoiced with her.

The true bride of Christ stood fearless as an unearthly beast emerged from the false bride's twisted countenance while her rage shifted from one face to the other. However, it was held back by the limitations of the darkness that held it. It could no longer pretend to be something other than what it was. Deception was its position of power. No pretended sweetness could defy the possession of the wrath that filled the two faces of the dirty, disheveled bride.

"You and I both know that your idolatry is being exposed and people are finally looking beyond your myths and lies for what is real," declared the true bride as she stood her ground. *"*Surely, y*ou can see that your fear and dread are losing their hold over people. You rely now on obvious hatred. And as you hate us and attack us, all I have to do is love them and you're facade will be stripped away. They can choose your Babylonian harlotry if they so prefer, but they will finally know you're not a real God!"*

Back and forth, the abomination's head tossed as her eyes rolled back into their sockets. Appearing less and less like anything human, an angry chorus of faces resembling all those who'd given her their power rose interchangeably between her two faces. She turned her head violently in front of the true bride as rage exploded from her mouth every level of degradation. Unimaginable profanity spewed forth from her like vomit directed at the true bride of Christ, only to be reflected by the Presence of heaven that repelled it like an arm casting aside unwanted rubbish.

Coarseness and cruelty broke forth from her like rats from an empty burning building. On and on, she continued to vent a demonic vulgarity that revealed her true intent of subverting and slandering the One True God. Rolling, foaming and writhing in uncontrolled waves of wrath, the false bride lashed out in fits of rage, filling the forest with her venom. But one movement from the glorious bride sent a tremor through her and all who attended her.

Watching breathlessly, Beloved saw this intensely powerful bride assume a steadfast stance against the onslaught of rage in front of her. Simply, yet profoundly, she held a large, gleaming bright, golden scepter in her hand. Driving it firmly into the ground, it silenced the harlot's demonic rage.

As the end of the scepter struck the darkness of the forest, shafts of glorious light shot out from all around it, pulsating throughout. Unfolding over the top of the dark lake, it bombarded the foliage of the surrounding woods, sending it reeling.

Displaying her rightful ascendancy to rule even in the darkest domains of the spirit-realm, the bride of the King of kings held in her the reminder of the ultimate demise of those who follow the accuser. Beloved felt the weight of the authority the bride displayed and was overcome with emotion over the historical importance of what was taking place.

Knowing full well she was Christ's true bride, Beloved couldn't help asking herself from where this powerful bride had come. *How is this possible?* Her mind swirled with questions as the two brides opposed each other.

The monster continued to heave her venomous slander, with pointless resolve. Instead of the effect she'd desired, no one was afraid of her. In fact, they marveled at her curiously instead. All the while, the stately bride stood her ground, unnerved by the relentless assault against her. Her glory became more obvious to even the most deceived beings in the dark forest.

As she was forced by the woman to display her sovereignty again and again in advancing degrees, the stronger the bride became. Each time she stood against the wrath of the false bride, the glory of heaven pounded against the captives in the dark lake. Again and again, they felt the presence of something that terrified them but they could not deny. It was the power of the Great One! Their Creator was reaching them through the tremendous battle of the two brides.

As the violence raged against the bride of Christ, the level of control that held them in bondage was weakening as the glory and reality of heaven was revealed. The veils of deception covering them began dissipating as the reality of their condition fell heavy on their conscious minds. With the lies of the accuser breaking, the captives were suddenly terrified as they began to understand the depth of their own bondage and realization of their own personal, desperate condition.

They were altogether terrified as they perceived the reality of God. All they could wonder was how terrifying their end would be. *If God is real,* they reasoned, *He must hate me.* They were filled with dread and shame…

Beloved had grown terribly weary from the tremendous battle she faced and did not realize the impact it was having on her. Her emotional state had sustained the overwhelming blows for sometime, but only Father realized her heart was heavier than she could stand. Falling wearily to the ground as the conflict continued, she lay limp. It was heaven's moment to refresh their young protege and, without raising notice, Arch-angel Michael recovered her from the battlefield, carrying her tattered heart back to his celestial home, where they could minister to her.

3

MICHAEL

MICHAEL FLEW ON his great warhorse toward heaven as Beloved lay against his chest, emotionally and physically exhausted. Drawing nearer, she saw tremendously ornate silver columns supporting massive gates covered by a mist of glory. Opening with great purpose and ceremony, it was as if the gate itself, standing tall and stately, were welcoming the great war-prince and his guest.

As they entered, she couldn't take her eyes off the majestic, towering, celestial gates. Craning her neck to see the towers rising above it, the doors opened like very large arms welcoming her into this glorious realm.

Entering the blessed kingdom, she quickly endeavored to take everything in. After entering through the first set of gates, she noticed another equally beautiful set further inside. Although it was similar to its outside counterpart, they stopped before entering the second pair of gates. Remaining in between the two heavenly gates, they were soon surrounded by a crowd of people who'd awaited their arrival.

While still atop the mighty steed, they were approached by a very beautiful woman whose name was Luminous. In response, Michael reached around to take Beloved's arm, lowering her down the side of his great horse. Standing separately from the crowd, it seemed the woman had been appointed for a special mission regarding Beloved.

All around them watched as Luminous embraced her like a mother embraces a well-loved child. Holding her a long while, Beloved felt healing power flow through her as the crowd watched in admiration. She began to cry as the peace and acceptance washed over her heart and mind. Wave after wave of healing power overflowed her spirit, cleansing her soul from the pain of accusation and slander that had followed her since she was a child.

This divinely graceful woman ministered to her as Love's enduring faithfulness washed over her, setting her free. As Beloved's sobs were finally comforted, the woman was presented with a tray of beautifully fresh strawberries and she responsively reached for some to offer her guest.

While Beloved was preoccupied by the attention from this blessed woman, she was unaware of Lord Jesus seeking out the attention of Arch-Angel Michael while both rested on their horses. *"General,"* He greeted him warmly.

Michael turned his attention to Him. *"Yes, my Lord,"* he answered.

"Has she given any indication that she is yet aware of who she is? Does she understand the reality of her mission?" Lord Jesus asked the great general.

Bowing his head in understanding, as they were all anxious for this event to occur, he responded, *"Sadly, my Lord, I still feel she is unaware of her true purpose. She's heard it all several times, but it's all the old wounds which keep her from truly receiving the truth of who she is."*

Turning his horse slightly, His gaze fell intently upon Michael. Lord Jesus retorted, *"Soon, General. We must get through to her soon. Much of our future plans are hanging in the balance."* He turned again to watch as Beloved recovered from her experience within the dark forest.

Michael nodded in agreement, as he resumed his vigilant manner.

Heavenly strawberries offered on a silver tray brought joy to Beloved's heart and, as she gratefully ate them she felt like a child refreshed by a lovely treat after her long cry. As her mind was refreshed, she looked around her at all the faces that were there to greet her.

For the first time, she was able to see Michael with perfect clarity and was amazed by him. He was magnificent, as he sat gloriously upon his horse. He was better than twelve feet tall and covered completely in hammered silver armor that fit him like a second skin. His helmet sported splendid wings protruding from either side. In his hand was an enormous scepter that rested firmly upon the ground. But most astounding of all was the breadth and size of his colossal wings. Stretched out and unfurled at his sides, they were muscular and powerful. Yet, their feathers appeared soft as silk while as lustrous and translucent as organza.

The warrior's prodigious warhorse matched his size perfectly. Standing attentively, even he seemed to understand the significance of the event taking place. He was a stunning dapple gray stallion with slips of silver wrapping his tail and mane, enhancing his regal appeal. It was obvious to all the affection the animal had for Beloved. As she approached him, he nestled her head with his muzzle, radiating tenderness.

The sound of stomping and clanging metal sent her twirling to face what she'd previously only glanced at. Astonished to see a mighty cavalry at attention, she was confronted by magnificent, heavenly warriors. Instinctively, she perceived she was meant to inspect this formidable army. Drawn to them by distinct feelings of familiarity, she apprehended their earnest friendship for her, and garnered curious strength from their presence.

Much like the warrior, Michael, they were armor-clad in silver regalia, yet were smaller than he. Although they were keenly aware of the honor and importance of their meeting with Beloved, she perceived they were incredibly eager to be released to fight in the significant battle for the Father's kingdom which lay ahead for them.

Mounted on a magnificent beast, Jesus spoke to her as He flanked the army. Turning instantly, she sought for the familiar source of the voice. It was He who was called *"Faithful and True"* and through seeing Him, she was made instantly serene.

Leaning down in order to speak more intimately, He spoke again to make sure she'd heard him. *"These gallant warriors are yours, Beloved. They will join you soon."*

Perplexed, she surveyed the vast army and asked, *"Why, Lord? Will I need them? I don't understand."*

"They're the army you asked Me to send to you, remember?"

Suddenly, she was taken back in her mind to her little home, years ago, in the midst of a dreadful demonic attack. She'd cried out for an army of angels seventy-feet thick.

"Yesss!" she shrieked. As she appraised the impressive army, she felt by the Spirit what they would go through for her. Her heart swelled with gratitude for their sacrifice.

"You can talk to them Beloved," He urged, knowing their enduring faithfulness to His kingdom should be acknowledged.

As she moved to speak with them, she was choked with emotional thanksgiving and relief for the answer to her prayer. While filled with sincere gratitude, she sidled alongside one horse nearer to her and stroked his face, her eyes fixed on its rider. *"Thank you,"* she said. Brimming with emotion, she was unable to say more, but it was enough.

Understanding the desperation in her heart, they were blessed by her gratitude.

Suddenly, the heavenly warhorse reared up on hind legs, stroking the air with its hooves. She felt his determination, like David standing before Goliath. His resolute spirit flooded her heart with thankfulness and her eyes with tears. Looking up at his grand gesture, she saw a single drop of glory spill from his hoof and fall on her face, filling her heart with heavenly splendour.

Indeed, she felt its effect earnestly and all the emotions she'd kept tucked away inside of her began to undo her resolve. She was terribly overwhelmed by it all and did not feel worthy. *"Why me?"* she asked the Lord.

Over and over, Lord Jesus articulated to Beloved, *"You are My BELOVED, in whom I AM well-pleased!"* until it sunk deep into her heart. Dismounting His great steed, Jesus knew He needed to work to make an impression on her, to show her she did not yet fully understand the mystery of her name. Ushering her to the side of a nearby pillar, He faced her straight away. Refusing to be hindered, He disarmed her with a silly grin, and held up a sign in front of her eyes that read, *"BELOVED!"*

Studying it, she brightened up immediately. *"I got it,"* she said pointing her finger up in the air! *"If you separate my name, BELOVED, you get BE LOVED. You want me to let You love me fully? Is that right?"*

"You cannot change the fact that you are Father's beloved, but you don't always feel loved. Isn't that right?" He asked her.

Soberly nodding her head, she answered, *"When the accusing voices come, it seems they want nothing but perfection, finding only fault. It wears away the certainty of Father's love and makes me feel as though I am unlovable."*

"They're trying to rob you, Beloved," He stated defiantly, *"and, if they could, they'd rob you of Father, Himself."*

She nodded again in sad agreement.

"But don't you see that it does not matter if we are unlovable, because His love is unconditional - there are NO CONDITIONS to His love. So, truly, it's not about feeling lovable because you could never do enough good to redeem yourself. It's about the fact that HE IS LOVE!"

"Father IS LOVE, Beloved, does that sound familiar to you? If we deny His love, we deny Him. The two cannot be separated - it is Who He is. It is His essence - His being. And when Father calls you BELOVED, He is doing more than trying to show you that He loves you. He is trying to help you receive His love and healing. He wants you to let yourself be loved by Him!"

Overwhelmed by emotion, Beloved dropped her face into her hands and let her tears flow. The overwhelming trials and fires of perpetual pain flooded her heart repeatedly. All she wanted was to love and be loved, but what she got was used and mistreated by those she wanted to bless.

Lord Jesus wrapped His arms around her and held her while she cried. He had meant to draw her out and help her see her true feelings. She needed healing and He knew only Father's love could do that.

"Years ago," Beloved shared as she regained her composure, *"I had a dream of heavenly Father. He was indescribable and so much more than I'd ever imagined Him to be. He was just what you were saying - He was LOVE. But,"* she turned again to the woman called Luminous, who was still by her side, *"even saying that now doesn't really describe Him. Our version of love and perfection is so different and it doesn't measure up to what He is. His love doesn't just tolerate us. It appreciates us. His love is like.. it is like a celebration!"* She looked up with wide eyes, discovering it for the first time. *"And when He sees you or even thinks about you, it's like His love just explodes with joy!"*

"That's why I represented His nature with the parable of the Prodigal Son (Luke 15:11-32)," Jesus interjected, *"because it is much more like that than anything else the world has been told."*

"Yeah," Beloved agreed, *"I feel like the miracle of my whole life will be just like that, 'When I was lost, He found me and while I was still a sinner, He still loved me and sent YOU to save me!'"* She pointed to the Lord. *"His love is relentless and He's continually pursuing us. But, I still struggle feeling it when the enemy attacks. And unless I can learn to receive it and to fully allow Him to love me... well, I*

just... I just have to learn to receive it, because I need it!"

"The closest person I can think of to describe Father's love is my own earthly father," Luminous joined in their conversation as she was very interested in Beloved's deliverance. *"He was the kind of person that left you in no doubt of his love. You absolutely felt loved when he loved you. He had the most enormous eyes and as blue as a summer sky. When he saw you, he would explode with celebration. He was so loud and would often pick me up and squeeze so tight I thought I might burst. He'd twirl me around and then sit me back down on my feet just to stand back and look at me with an expression of celebratory pride."*

"Sometimes," she continued, *"I think of him now with Heavenly Father. They have so much in common. Father God has the most amazing, piercing eyes, filled to overflowing with excited jubilation when He sees you, Beloved. And when He finally gets you to receive His love, He wants nothing more than to pick you up and squeeze you so tight, dancing with the glee of celebrating you! And surely, He, too, sets you back down on your own two feet just to stand back and look at who you are, overwhelmed with satisfaction. And every time you wake up, He loves you. When you're exhausted, He loves you. When you're cranky, He loves you even more. And when you pull yourself back up one more time after you have fallen again, He loves you to tears as you return to Him. He loves you so much that I think His greatest pain must come to Him when you won't let Him love you like He wants to. It must be painful for Him when we turn and go our own way, when we entangle ourselves in sins that weigh down our heart and make us run from His forgiveness instead of to it. Don't you agree?"* She looked to Beloved for agreement.

"Several years back," Beloved was ready with a reply, *"I had a run-in with someone and they hurt me very badly. I felt so unloved, so contemptible and horrid. I thought it would be a long time before I could stop feeling the self-hatred their condemnation brought. After a difficult night's sleep, I woke up the next morning and, before remembrances of the previous day could hit me, I felt Father's Holy Presence singing to me."*

"He was singing a song I'd heard that I liked, and, when He sang, it took on a whole new meaning. The words were 'You're amazing, just the way you are!' After all they'd said to me, His words washed over and over and I felt His acceptance

through that silly song. I thought, even if no other human soul in the world loves or approves of me, there is nothing on Earth that could measure His love!" She shook her head as she started to break down again, but this time from the massive weight of His love for her.

"Indeed, Beloved," Luminous commiserated with her, *"people can devastate your soul, and strip you of your equilibrium. Our own human failure, too, can leave us unhappy with ourselves. None of that changes the fact that the Almighty God of the universe, who created the mountains, oceans and deserts, as well as us, loves us that much! You are His GRAND FINALE, sweetheart."* She smiled sweetly.

"He made you to love you, Beloved. He imagined you and loved you before you were even born. And all of heaven celebrates with Him. They cheered when you took your first steps and rejoiced when you finally turned to Lord Jesus for the first time and the second and third and millionth!" She smiled and couldn't help but lean in and give her a hug as she saw Beloved's eyes grow misty.

"The serpent's greatest victory is to convince a human soul that God is not loving, that He's harsh and demanding. Or that, if He is love, you won't

qualify for it," Jesus interjected. *"But no other dreadful lie is more hated by Father than this, because the exact opposite is true. It was because He loved the world that He sent Me, His only Son, as a sacrifice to save it. His love is much better than anyone on Earth could imagine and He wants none to perish but for all to find and have eternal life in Me (John. 3:16).*

"The world can hate you, your parents can abandon you, but none of that disqualifies you from God's love - it doesn't even come close! Beloved, you are surely, and truly and absolutely adored." He stood again, holding His sign, imploring her to *Be Loved!* Pointing to it with an open grin, He worked to make her laugh until He succeeded.

4

ABIDE IN ME

SEVERAL DAYS LATER, Beloved was resting in her prayer garden back on Earth when a small bird flew down next to her and mounted a dramatic display of emotional discourse, all played out with his wings while tweeting his excitement. It occurred to her that this creature wished for her to follow it and, not yet being able to turn down a creature in distress, she acquiesced.

As bird's fly much faster than human's can walk, their journey together tried the bird's patience. At last, they came to a grouping of large, arched trees so dense she could barely see their outline.

The bowed trees grew into a long gallery of twisted branches and vines woven together, arching to make an enticing, secret passageway.

Beloved was captivated by the trees and had succumbed to the charm of the sweet, earthy fragrance of the hidden corridor when her attention was caught by the sight of her new little friend motioning with a flutter for her to hurry.

Continuing to follow, she sensed this journey carried more importance than what she'd originally thought. What had appeared to be just an adventurous romp through the woods was now becoming an experience, which she noticed was making mysterious alterations in her. Though she was puzzled how it could be so, her hateful long-time companion, rejection, was loosing his grip on her heart and fresh hope was dawning in her mind. She was beginning to understand she was not what the voices of rejection had made her out to be. She was, indeed, who Heavenly Father declared her to be.

Rushing to keep in pace with her little companion, she drank in quick glimpses of her surroundings as they journeyed through a tunnel of bliss-filled greenery. Possessing the pure innocence of a small child, this beautiful place held a level of purity she wanted to explore further.

Worldliness looks down on places like this, she thought, *but what a treasure it is. How can they comprehend the wealth of innocence and the lightness it brings to your mind when such a dark veil has lain over their consciousness? How can they understand without being shown?*

"Wait for me," she cried out to the little bird, who flew on impatiently.

Resting upon a branch to let her catch up with him, it wasn't long before he was off again and out of sight, for, the layers of trees overhead were thickening and the branches were narrowing, creating a much shorter ceiling in the tunnel. Now crouching, the passage was too short for her, yet perfect for agile little birds.

As she neared the end of the passageway, Beloved thought her adventure was ending. But her guide flew without stopping to the very end of the tunnel. Soon, she realized he was studying something in the brush.

Covered by the thickness of the greenery, she saw a small opening with branches she was just able to pull aside. Behind it, was a simple wooden door. Clearly ancient, the door opened on its own as her little friend flew inside. As she quickly followed behind him, the passage was just large enough for her to squeeze through.

Presently, she found herself in a warm, appealing room that possessed everything an intimate little home would. It's indulgent decor made the room inviting. At the center were excessive pillows of colorful material that surrounded a square wooden table only a foot off the floor.

The room radiated comfort and peace, but her greatest discovery was that of angels surrounding the perimeter who filled it with brilliant light. Hidden from the outside world, you would never know such a place existed. She understood that not many people came here and her presence was special.

Turning again to her little guide, she stumbled back a step as she realized he'd grown dramatically in size and was now all of six feet tall. No longer a small bird, he had become a towering eagle. Indeed, he must be the Great Eagle she'd heard others speak of.

He reached out his wings and wrapped Beloved in them, embracing her as if his hug were the purpose of her visit there. Feeling the most intense power emitting from him, it filled the room. Opening her heart like nothing she'd ever felt before, it broke down the toughness she'd allowed to callous her heart in an effort to protect herself. Suddenly, she perceived in herself a heightened sense of insight and understanding that made the pain of her past a dim memory.

A secret place of revelation and impartation, this majestic place was the eagle's nest. Now that she had full understanding of why they had journeyed there, she was able to relax. Showing her around the room, the Great Eagle shared with her His private treasures and pictures that He seemed especially proud of. Even the angelic joined in and shared the joyous prizes the Great Eagle cherished but was too humble to speak of. Before she realized it, hours passed by and all knew she must leave soon.

The angelic turned to her, saying, *"Lord Jesus is waiting for you, Beloved. He has much more to show you. He wanted you to receive your gifting from the Great Eagle, so you would have understanding of what He was to reveal. Now is the time for you to depart, but we've so enjoyed our time with you. We hope this will be the first of many visits."* They continued to wish her well, giving her hugs for her journey.

Wrapped in the eagle's wings, this time they shot straight through the ceiling. She had enjoyed herself a great deal and was filled with misgivings about leaving such a precious place. But if Lord Jesus needed her, that was where she wanted to be.

* * *

Beloved's journey with the eagle had led her again to a peaceful garden brimming with green. Nestled in the back of a small secluded outdoor room, she was pleasantly surprised to find Lord Jesus waiting patiently for her on a bench. Although He greeted her warmly, He seemed somewhat solemn. His eyes were filled with a heavy weight, but also great love for her.

After studying His demeanor, she noticed what she thought might be the purpose of the meeting. In His hands, he was carefully holding a tiny sprig of a plant about three to four inches long.

Raising up the branch to let her see it clearly, He told her, *"This is you, Beloved,"* acknowledging it with a nod of His head. He raised up His open hand to show her the scar He bore from the crucifixion and, at the same time, seated the bottom of the branch into the scar of His hand.

Deeply moved by His message, she began to cry, for suddenly His entire arm became one seamless branch. Blending perfectly, as though it had always been conjoined, He revealed His purpose to her. *"Beloved,"* He said, *"Abide in Me."*

Then He picked up another branch from an oak tree which had been completely covered in gold. Turning and twisting it, it became a crown He placed gently on her head. *"You, My Beloved, are indeed crowned with the oaks of righteousness."*

He took from a small leather pouch a large seven-strand pearl necklace. Putting it around her neck with great purpose, He said, *"You, My dear, have created every one of these pearls through the trials and pains you've endured for My sake."* And, truly, it was clear that each pearl had been wrought through great trauma and trial, but was now something of great beauty.

Head heavier now, with eyes downcast, Jesus reached down and pulled a scroll out of the ground and held it in His hands as if He were building up the strength to hand it to her. By and by, He asked her to taste it. With a curious nod, Beloved took it from His hands and raised the scroll to her mouth.

As the scroll was tasted, she instantly began to weep, overwhelmed by the sorrow she felt in it. He waited tenderly for her to compose herself, then steadied Himself with a demeanor of great purpose. *"Beloved, you must prepare yourself and make yourself ready for what is to come upon the earth."*

"Up until now, I have only been your hobby. Now, however, I must become your life. Every choice you make must be My choice and every step you take, My step. For the path you enter will be thwarted with obstacles. The enemy has sown deceit into My work and caused many before you to stumble. History will speak of your faithfulness to Me, My Beloved, and I want your story to shine for generations to come."

She felt a tinge of painful disappointment in herself, suddenly understanding the that distractions in her life must come to an end. No longer could she afford to be controlled by others and their opinions. She must trust her own ear. Obedience and deference to this precious Man would be the only safe path ahead.

Without hesitation, His demeanor changed dramatically and was markedly stern. His countenance was filled with the authority of the Ancient of Days as He drew His sword from His side and struck it into the ground. *"Beloved, you are one of My eagles and I am counting on you. It is now time to prepare yourself for war!"*

"If you shine your light as I ask, you will gain the world's attention. The cruelty of the masses will turn its attention to your light. Those who pretend to be Christians but are actually working for My enemies will try to destroy you and dim your light. Take comfort, for all the darkness in the world will suddenly be exposed as My Truth rises in radiance!

"You've been told countless things that have made it difficult for you to understand your purpose or how you are to fulfill your mission. You've been wounded by accusation and slander. Yet, you are not what they say you are. You are powerful, fruitful, kind and self-sacrificing.

"Indeed, Beloved, you are much more powerful and fearless than you could ever imagine.

"However, you've lost your way and the woundedness you've suffered has caused your heart to grow bitter. You tried to endure and be who mankind said you should be, but you became afraid and discouraged. The bitterness of your heart opened you up to danger and made you vulnerable

to the designs of the enemy. Your vulnerability has caused the enemy to rise up in presumptive aggression against you and they've been made fearless in their boldness to ruin you.

"However, they do not realize that I've allowed them to war against you because I needed you to know who you are in Me. I needed you to recognize your power and purpose in Me and, in fighting them, you found Me as your Cornerstone. You are alive in this hour because I knew that when you finally realized who you are, you would walk with Me in the authority I've given you. You will become the light I knew you would become.

"My church is the most powerful force on the earth, but they do not know it yet. There are voices trying desperately to restore the heart of My church, but they are being viciously attacked. They are declaring the power of My kingdom, My favor and My love, but the wolves have tried to gobble them up with slander and accusation.

"As your enemies rage against you, you will need to know who you are. Do not allow the darkness to lead you - you are the light!

"Yes, truly the world is dark - that is why I need you! But, there are many in My church who are not

*Mine but are only pretending. Indeed, they belong to the enemy and work for him. Sadly, they've led many astray. They pretend to be hurt, needing help, and the weakness of compassion unchecked has given them an open door to destroy many with their deluded dark powers. Compassion is good, but it is imperative that it is guided by My discernment. Heed My voice. Do no let unbridled compassion lead you. Do not believe everyone who says they've been hurt and need your help. Your mission is not to help everyone you meet, but you are here to obey Me. Follow only My leading. **This is very important**.*

"Darkness and despair have overtaken the people of the earth, yet MY GLORY will rise upon YOU! You are here to shine! You are the light of the world - like a city on a hilltop that cannot be hidden. No one lights a lamp and then puts it under a basket. Instead, a lamp is placed on a stand where it gives light to everyone in the house. In past, I've kept you hidden, but now you need to shine your light for all to see, so that everyone will praise and love heavenly Father because of you.

"Truly, I've called you to be My ambassador and your light comes from Me, from My home. As you live in ME, your light will be unquenchable and

piercingly bright, penetrating the darkness of the earth. Dear One, I've prepared you for this hour to reveal the power I've given to My church and to prepare the way for Me.

"As you decree and declare My miraculous power, do NOT shy away from declaring My Gospel to the nations! Declare BOLDLY My love for mankind! Though the darkness rages against you, do not fear it. As you stand for My love, you may feel small and vulnerable, but I will give you the words to speak that will disarm the hostility of the darkness. They are truly hungry and will be moved by your persistence to win them. Your steps must be sure and certain for you have only My strength to save you from their anger.

"Every step they take toward you with the intent to destroy you will cool the hatred that possesses them. Do not respond to their anger, but reveal to them who they truly are as I give you the words to speak. They think they are coming after you because they hate you, but really I am sending them to you because they are so lost in the emptiness of their crippled heart and the wounds created from living in darkness.

"Remember they have been lied to and they, too, have been told they are someone they are not.

They've felt noble in their hatred of you. It's become their dark purpose and has even come to define what they believe is their existence.

"As you begin to tell them who they really are and the purposes they were created for, you will see for yourself the purposes for which I've destined you to fulfill. You will discover the answers you were looking for. I will make it obvious to you; you will not miss it.

"I've given you My love for them and this love is your armor to defend against the hostility that holds them captive. You can trust My love; it will melt their defensiveness.

"As their heart is restored to them, the hunger for the light that is hidden inside them will emerge and the darkness that has encased them will fall away. Even you will be surprised by what you will see in them. Their humanity will come forth and take your breath away.

"Like a mother, you will feel a supernatural connection to them and want to care for them. As they grow in My strength and their purpose is revealed, you will stand back in awe of what you have done for My kingdom. My light will produce great fruitfulness in them and they will transform the world around them. The water of My Word and

the light of My Spirit will become their best friends as they are made brand new!

"As though they have been awakened from a deep slumber, they will, in turn, administer My power to those around them and will consume the darkness that envelopes those with them. Their fruitfulness will spread as My abundant life renews their humanity, overwhelming the darkness.

"You were created for this moment. You are a carrier of My Presence! Let My heart flow through you! I've given you the nations as your inheritance - they are your treasure! This treasure will last for eternity and you will no longer be rejected, but overwhelmed by acceptance."

Raising her head toward Him, eyes filled with tears, Beloved could muster only a simple *"Yes"* through a voice heavy with gratitude, penance and love.

"Father and I have have prepared another surprise for you," He continued, *"It is well that you journey to the far-side of Father's mountain. We have something there you will enjoy,"* giving her a hug, He sent her on her way with the brightest smile, exuding love for her.

Waving goodbye, Beloved didn't want to leave Him, but even more-so, she wanted to make Him proud.

As she turned to the Great Eagle, they set off together again.

5

THREE HORSES

SENT TO THE far side of heavenly Father's mountain, Beloved was unsure of why the Lord had insisted on her journey to this distant place. He'd spoken to her heart and explained He had something special to reveal, but she had no idea how desolate it would be. As she was unacquainted with the area herself, Great Eagle had accompanied her to this lonely place. Stumbling over jagged rocks, Beloved fell and landed on a pile of vines and brush. She felt her hand strike something hard as she reached to catch herself, and heard the crack of wood giving way a bit.

Full of curiosity, Beloved dug past the vines and found an old sign buried under the brush. She cleared it off and read just one word, *"SURRENDER." Surrender? What on Earth?* she asked herself. Looking all around, she realized it must have come from somewhere up above as she caught sight of a rusted nail still in an old decaying vine.

Her mind went in all directions, wondering what it was for and who'd left it. But what did it mean? Was it a warning of some kind? Setting it on the nail again, she walked on, struggling to keep up with the hurried pace of the Great Eagle.

After meeting the eagle she'd heard so much about, Beloved was so grateful for his company. She had always felt his strength and it gave her great confidence to lean on him. As though leading her, he flew ahead and landed upon the roof of a desolate shack. Turning, he faced the mountain range and proceeded to watch for something.

Though Beloved was unfamiliar with everything on this side of the mountain, he appeared to be very acquainted with it. Dark and uninviting, the mountain suddenly seemed formidable. A storm was forming over the mountain's peak and she sensed in her spirit it would change everything.

Darkness made the air damp and the atmosphere ominous. She'd always felt comfortable with the mountain of God, but this region revealed there was so much more about Father she had yet to learn.

Who is this God of mine? she pondered.

The courage of the eagle emboldened her to carry herself with bravery. But just as she reached the shack upon which he'd perched, she was thrown off balance by a shaking underfoot. Reacting in shock, she grasped futilely at the air for support. Despite the weakening of her knees, Beloved managed to keep upright until her hands found their way around one of the splintered posts holding up the dilapidated porch at the front of the shack.

Just in time, she was braced for the impact of the quake as it grew in intensity. The brittle wooden structure seemed inadequate for a refuge from such a powerful force, but she'd have to trust it to keep her, for there was no time to find anything else. The presence and confident stillness of the eagle reassured her, so she kept her ground.

Feeling assured of her own safety, she returned her attention to the mountain. It convulsed with threatening energy. Spitting out pieces of itself, it shook violently, as smoke rose from the back of the great summit.

"Lord!" her heart leapt in amazement. *"What is happening here? Are You with me?"*

She clung to the hope that all she was enduring was God's doing. He had led her here and she trusted He would see her through.

Suddenly, the earth around her was hit by a tremendous blast and Beloved was thrown back once again against the old structure. Something had given way. The explosion had set off a surge of smoke and flashes of light from the side of the mountain. Fire and ash roared up into the night sky. Bits of broken rock and embers shot out, awakening the darkness with the fire's light. Caught by the wind, the flames danced through the darkness, lighting up the mountain with fury.

Roaring, snapping, bursting, the mountain surrendered itself to the flames and propelled the fire upward until it breached the night sky. It was an exhibition of light that pervaded the night with a formidable invasion of illumination.

Again, the ground shook violently and Beloved braced herself with the remains of the shack's porch. Her shock turned to dread as she watched the side section of Father's great mountain burst forth and shoot itself high into the night, rolling out into the countryside a great distance. Instantly, the fire roared through the breach and blew off a good portion of rock, displacing a massive egress.

Great Eagle stood unamazed by what was taking place, as if he'd expected it - wanted it to happen. Without shielding himself or taking refuge, the eagle was unmoved by the explosions, as he sat perched on the roofline of the small wooden structure.

Beloved couldn't help but wonder if he was watching for something, for he looked as if he could see right into the side of the mountain's new opening and waited for what was yet to come.

Following the expectancy in his gaze, Beloved regarded the incident with new eyes. All at once, three grand horses emerged from the open cavern in gaited unison. Breaking out into the night, their exit seemed to restore peace, as if the shaking had given birth to what had come forth.

As the lead horse cantered toward Beloved, her heart leapt from her chest with astonishment. Without even considering herself, she ran out to meet it. His body was jet black, sleek and beautiful, and at first she thought he was just an ordinary horse. However, his head was extraordinary and made her draw back in awe. Though, it was admittedly a beautiful animal, it possessed the head of a great oxen.

Unusually large and muscular, his demeanor was quite bold. It seemed to Beloved from the first moment he was released on the earth that he proclaimed continuously, *"Come to Me, all who are weary and have heavy burdens to bear, and find rest in Me!"*

As she investigated the creature's path, it seemed to walk aimlessly throughout the earth, yet his journey was strategic and had a great purpose. As he called out to the earth, he pulled behind him a giant plow. Cutting deep into the dry land, it implanted a hungry spirit of repentance into the fallow ground.

The second horse had the head of a lion who possessed the fullest mane Beloved had ever seen. Shaking his head, he filled the earth with concentrated peace. He too was beautiful, and she realized he was released to the earth to bring an understanding and an appreciation for the fear of the Lord.

Through the Spirit, Beloved saw his destiny as he devoured the history books of man, releasing the season of the Cross on the earth, which she knew would be a brand new start for the church. Truly, they would understand the true power in the cross of Jesus! Like a baby, they would begin to walk as He'd always known they would. The Cross would be their battle cry, their anthem. And as they fought for the kingdom of heaven, it would be their victory!

She watched as people tried to ride upon his back, but his message was clear: he knew who was truly his and who was not. There would be no more knavery in the church. No more would people say they spoke for Him who didn't know Him. No more would they distract His people from His presence. The robbing, manipulation and bullying of God's children would be brought to an end, as through this horse, a greater level of discernment would be poured out on them.

The third horse had the head of an eagle and he represented a multitude of eagles released upon the earth. With white smooth feathers adorning him, the eagle comforted those who were distressed, but he also brought a tremendous fire to the earth. Everywhere the eagle went, he purified the church from all dross and true Christians rejoiced in his work. Beloved also saw by the Spirit that many ministries would fall under his fire. Though all seemed lost, what remained was genuine. The eagles taught the great importance of the Lordship of God, bringing fear to many ministries who served the god of ministry instead of ministering to the One True God. Sadly, they'd enjoyed the praise of man too much, and refused to surrender to His Lordship.

Beloved knew the three horses were to be the continued work of the church reformers and the fulfillment of Scripture, *"May your Kingdom come soon. May your will be done on earth, as it is in heaven."* (Matthew 6:9-10) Surely, this was the destination of the reformation. As she knew reformation had not yet been completed. These glorious creatures would bring the needed preparation for the emergence of Father's kingdom. For, as in heaven, His will is His government and, to have His government on earth, we must receive His will as more than mere suggestion. Indeed, Father has the right to govern His creation and His love for us should be enough to inspire our assured loyalty and surrender. Through these great beasts, He was answering the prayers of His people!

6

THE GREAT
EAGLE SPEAKS

THE WEIGHTINESS AND mystery of the three horses lay heavily on Beloved's heart until she was reminded of the closeness of the Great Eagle. Hadn't he been sent by Father to bring her comfort and give her needed understanding? *Yes,* she reasoned. *He will explain it all.*

As she turned to him, he seemed to have already anticipated the confusion of her heart and was awaiting her need of him.

"Beloved, Father is impatient for those who are His to truly know Him. What is about to manifest upon the earth will refine the church. Specifically, the prophets - little and great. Ever so much more will He reveal His justice to those who call themselves His but are snakes in disguise. One thing He will not tolerate are those who speak for Him but do not know Him. They are charlatans, and lead His children away from Him, and to themselves. Indeed, like the great deceiver, they want to be worshiped.

"All will become a target for what He is releasing, but, as some will bend to Father's will and repent, others will break under the weight of their stubborn hearts.

"Beloved," the eagle continued, *"Father has seen the confusion caused by those who call themselves prophets, yet are, at best, disingenuous. Many of them say they speak for Him but promote themselves instead. They see ministry as a career instead of a journey with Father. It's become a stench instead of a blessing and true prophets suffer from it. Like you, Beloved, those who follow Him will recognize the voice of a pretender when they hear it, but many are deceived by them and He has seen the pain caused by this.*

"Indeed, a new season is coming to the earth and preparation is needed. Reformation is still at work. Many more reformers, young and old, will rise up and speak for Father alone and will set the church aflame. You will see miracles through them, but the greatest and most advanced miracle will be the work of great cleansing in His house. Repentance will come like a wave upon the souls of men - first the church, then the unsaved.

"No longer will He put off the cries for justice. Those who've lost their lives for His sake will be remembered. Restitution will come to them as He reforms His house, then they will finally be satisfied!

"Precious Beloved, eagles are here to comfort and protect. However, we're also vessels of fire and we too will release His Holy Fire on the earth. Those who surrender to it will be transformed. However, not all will surrender. Sadly, some will turn away in defiance. Rebellion must bow, for Father will not share His glory with idol worshipers!

"This is wonderful news," the eagle reasoned. *"He is coming to us. He is coming to His house again. He will remove the old slag and pour out His*

effervescent joy on all of us, and those who seek Him will find Him."

"I have tried so hard to be continually filled with His Presence," Beloved sighed heavily. *"I wanted to make Him known."*

"You have been diligent, I know." The eagle was moved by her sentiments. *"Sadly, the church has tried to make God conform to their thinking, instead of the other way around, and many would not receive Him because of it. But now, Beloved, we will make Him known. We will share what we know of Him, and those He is calling will realize this is what they've been looking for."*

Beloved listened wide-eyed as the eagle continued, *"Father is seeking those whose heart yearns for Him more than they want the praise-of-man so He can pour through them His Holy Power.*

"Don't worry, Beloved. He has not forgotten the promises He has made to you. He is for you and will give you a sign of His favor - that is His delight."

Surrendering to tears again, Beloved was grateful to receive the affirmation of Father's feelings for her.

Turning away, the eagle gazed off and his demeanor altered slightly, as though he were not present with her anymore. He then continued,

"Father God did not give anyone authority to supplant His prophets the way they have. They think it is simple to copy them and misappropriate their mission, but the anointing of the prophets cannot be copied, for they are so much more to Father than the sum of their prophesies.

"Indeed, it's the motives of their hearts and the seasoning of the Spirit that makes them valuable. The price they've paid to know Him has been high and their journey deeply painful, yet they've surrendered to it gladly. As they've battled the onslaught of the enemy's continuous hatred of them, they've become golden in their understanding of Father. No, Beloved, this cannot be copied and those who follow Jesus will know and feel the presence of Father's treasure and value it.

"Heavenly Father continuously calls to those who would be His, saying: 'Come to Me and turn away from deception. I will reward you with My sure Word... a Word from My heart. Come to Me, those who are Mine. Come out from the world and seek My face alone. I alone can give you the life that you seek. Come and I will fill your empty heart. Turn away from the favor of man, and seek Me for My favor.'

"Those who've answered His calling will not be recognized by the world, but the enemy knows who they are. They are not flashy, but they shine just the same. Truly, those who have been with Father are unassuming and unremarkable by human reasoning, but will be known by the fruit of Wisdom Himself."

Deep in thought, Beloved stared up at the night sky while taking in all the eagle had conveyed to her.

"It is a shame, isn't it?" she finally spoke.

"Shame, Beloved?"

"Yes," she answered. *"It would be a dreadful shame to waste one's life on ministry, thinking one was doing the work of the Lord, only to find in the end they were working for ministry's sake alone and missing the true purpose of it."*

"Indeed," the eagle responded. *"We should be careful of planting seeds that will harvest no fruit. Only in the Father will we find what we've been looking for. Ministry is a response to finding Him.*

"In past, I often heard Father urging His reformers to surrender to His judgment as often as they are offered, for in them they experienced a love greater than they ever knew existed. Beloved, this is your hour to know Father as He truly is. Indeed, you are weary. You've tried to labor in the Spirit,

but you keep falling back into your own strength. Surrender to the ministry of His yoke. This is imperative. Your time in His Presence will transform you and change every aspect of your life. Abide in His love for you and your enemies will run from you.

"Repentance leads you straight to Father's heart and into His Presence. If you give your labor to Him and surrender yourself, He will cover you with a banner of love to enter the secret place. Remember, Beloved, He wants to belong to you as well as having you for His own.

"Many on Earth pray and plead to have Father's will be done on the earth. Yet, what they do not understand is that, unless they experience Him, they will not understand His will. As you say 'yes' to Him, His will becomes a part of your heart. It will overwhelm your life with the strength of purpose you crave. It shakes off the selfish plans that are only a distraction. For your weakness is a desire to always be doing important things for Him, but that is not how His kingdom works. What is not surrendered to the kingdom of God, will always be vulnerable to the control of this world and those who want to sideline your purpose."

"I have always wanted to be sure my life mattered," Beloved interjected. *"I don't want to miss the mark. I've let others tell me what God wants me to do, because I didn't trust myself. And I have seen the deceptive power of measuring myself to them. Father's always told me, 'Those who will live for My delight will know My voice.' It's true, too. It seems the more He has disciplined and humbled me, the greater my love for Him grows - the hungrier for Him I become."*

"And..." the eagle interrupted, *"the more you understand just how much He loves you."*

"I've seen Him refine the reformers in what I thought must be relentless fire," Beloved continued, *"but it seems they bore it beautifully. They almost welcome His discipline and pruning! I'm not sure if I'm there yet. I've fallen short so many times."*

"Falling short is important too, Beloved," the eagle responded. *"If you didn't, you'd be unreliable in battle. Because, as Moses disobeyed when he struck the rock, we can become too accustomed to success. Unrighteous judgment like hateful daggers has risen against the church, and those who hate are guilty of the sin of murder. Their pride will lead to their humiliation unless they submit to the authority of the Christ. Those who know Jesus as*

Lord and Ruler will stand out as boldly as a lily in the desert. The more we bend to His will, the more effective we'll become in this hour."

"Your struggle with anger comes from weariness," he continued. *"Your battle has been difficult and long. You have wondered sometimes if Father has forgotten you, or that somehow something you have done has negated the promises He has made to you, but He has always been with you. He is your Source and He has been supplying your endurance. It's time for you to rejoice in the victories He has given and fight for those yet to come. Your mission is faith when all hope is lost. Beloved, you are a warrior and you're learning to trust!*

"You have been set apart for this hour, and it is time for you to rise! You will prepare the church for the hour they are about to enter. They need truth and understanding - they need to know the Father. They have been lied to and what they think they know will lead them to ruin. It is time for them to love Him as He is!

"You don't want to believe in yourself, but what choice do you have? Don't worry - Father will never deny your contrite heart. Come now; let me

provide shelter for you under my wings. It's time to ask the Father to send you an ARMY!"

7

FIRE ARMY

BELOVED WAS EXHAUSTED after the day's events, and easily fell asleep on the old cabin's floor as the Great Eagle watched over her. Even so, her slumber was not dreamless and soon her sleep was captivated by visions of a mysterious dark creature approaching her. Wearing a cape, it was hidden, yet she saw its shoulders were covered in a marvelous scale-like armor. But peering down at its feet, she was surprised to find it possessed the legs of a horse.

Suddenly, the creature forced back its head and whinnied into the atmosphere. Flames of fire exploded from its mouth, covering the expanse. It seemed determined to scorch everything around it, heaving a blaze of torrid breath from his mouth.

Beloved's vision cleared to reveal a fearsome beast of a horse, upon Whom rode an awe-inspiring Rider. This, she recognized, was the Lord. His eyes were flames of fire, His hair was ablaze and even the mane of the great creature He sat upon was burning. The horse and Rider were as black as though they had both been utterly scorched by fire.

As if taken prisoner by the fires of hell, they were not consumed but were made fearsome with its seasoning. Indeed, having championed over fire, they were now possessed of the elements of fire, making them defiantly intrepid. For surely, this magnificent Rider and His steed - together becoming a grave weapon to devour their adversary - would deliver those held in captivity. Though surrounded by the flames of hell, heaven had swallowed them up in its glory, protecting them from harm.

Standing beyond the awe-inspiring pair, Beloved now saw what lay to the far side of them. Following the Lord, she could see what appeared to be a sea of riders. All were equally changed as the Lord had been. Being transformed, they were a company of champions - an exceedingly distinguished ARMY OF FIRE!

Beloved felt, more than heard, the voice of an angel invade her dream, saying, *"They are not afraid of death because they have already died to their flesh. These are they who've fought carnality and won."*

Looking as though they would soon meet their end, she was shocked as she beheld the severity of their burns. However, what seemed fatal brought them no lasting harm. Rather, it made them fearless. For, transformed by fire, they were sodden in fury that left them undiluted and unaffected by the world.

Utterly terrifying, the existence of this tremendous army generated a formidable transformation in the atmosphere around them. Surely, they would be a terror to any enemy who encountered them. Yet, it was their enemies who'd created them. It was hell, itself, who'd trained this devastating force. Indeed, they'd endured all the fire hell could immerse them in. But, instead of annihilation, they'd been transformed by the glory fires of heaven - tried by fire, then anointed in Glory!

All at once, Beloved understood what she was seeing and was flooded with elation. It had been a long time since she'd seen them and they were almost unrecognizable. Surrendered to Father's will, they were now a great army, but she knew them as the PROPHETIC HOST! This was the army for which Lord Jesus had planned and prepared, choosing each individual warrior Himself with tremendous care. Indeed, they were the Lord's dear friends, who had endured years of intense training, testing and fire. Mighty, illustrious and noble, these were those of mankind of whom it was said, *"They loved not their lives even unto the death."* *(Revelation 12:11)* This was the army of Revival Fire!

Indeed, all of heaven longed for the manifestation of this tremendous host to emerge prepared for war, for with them would come a gathering of the harvest. And the fire of the Holy Presence accompanying them would burn away the veil of deception covering much of the church and world.

Truly, nothing in this world could take possession of them. All that had bound them was destroyed by intense trials of fire from their enemy. An undeniable love for their King had taken hold of them. Their temporal life on this earth was a mere implement in the Lord's hands, a sacrifice they chose to lay down at His feet as His passion consumed them.

Gleefully forfeiting their previous identities, they were now fused together with Father and King, living lives of fearsome power, yet hidden with Christ in God. As His conquering army of light, they lived for the glory of their King and His kingdom. It was the Lord's army. Plainly and utterly unstoppable, no defense could be mounted against it, for their battle had already been won as they had surrendered to Father's will.

Beloved awoke from the dream with an exhilarated heart. This was the army she'd prayed for and also the prophetic host she missed dearly. Yet, as she dwelt on it, an encroaching heaviness resisted her joy. She wondered what this would mean, and what possible cost it would require.

She recalled that her Lord's church had barely been three hundred years old before Satan had mounted a sneak attack against it. Unable to annihilate it with intense persecution, he'd supplanted it with a pretentious copy. Driving the true followers of Christ to hide for their lives, he replaced the church of the Christ with a Babylonian-pagan church. The Roman government, bent on world domination, introduced centuries of bloodshed and trauma in the name of Christ, while replacing Christ's Gospel story with myth, legend and idolatry. Indeed, so much had been lost, and, for twelve-hundred years, the Word of God was held captive. Even those who would read it in secret would be martyred.

However, just like prisoners held captive by a lion, one day the prisoners took the lion captive. Truth was fought for and won, but at a terrible price. Now, only five-hundred years later, would they be waging war for it again?

Indeed, it was the same in her day. Working under a veil of deceit, the enemy was confident in his intended victory and continued to believe in his contrived agenda. The church had taken for granted the suffering of the early reformers, and the evil they fought against was still lurking around the church like a panther waiting to strike its prey.

While scorning God, they mocked the light, embracing the depths of evil. Honestly believing Satan could conquer God, they put all their trust in this evil pretender. Yet, God had seen evil rising against His church and had prepared a generation of reformers to combat it.

So many of Father's children have been taken captive by darkness while still believing they follow the light, she thought uneasily, *and have become a part of the hordes of hell. Speaking out the same dreaded evil as those who worship the prince of darkness, they spread his hate and slander against us. How could they NOT think they would win?*

"Stop it, Beloved," she scolded herself aloud.

They have everything and we have nothing...

"Aaaah...but God." She smiled.

Then it occurred to her. Their unbelief and hatred left them vulnerable to underestimating God and blinded them to His power. Yes, He was ALMIGHTY GOD, after all. The reality wasn't that they were out-numbered - they did not live in accordance to the world's reality, but of heaven's. Endeavoring to saturate the world with evil, their enemies worked strenuously to stomp out God's Holy Word. Yet, they could not defeat Him!

"Yes," she responded, *"thank God! Thank God we have an army of fire starters! This is not a time of dread,"* she reasoned, *"for it is the end of the hour of the reign of darkness and the beginning of the hour of the Lord's triumphant church!"*

With a satisfied sigh, she surrendered to sleep once again.

8

WIND AND FIRE

"I WILL NOT be afraid of the terror by night, nor of the arrow that flies by day," Beloved repeated to herself, forcing her courage to rise as she awoke to the realization of a coming storm.

A large cloud of dust furled toward the old cabin at dangerous speed as she struggled to throw off the residue of sleep and adjust her mind to this new plight. *"What on the earth is happening?"* she screamed.

She looked around for some place safe to take cover and, leaving the cabin, she scrambled in the direction of the mountain of the Lord. *"Where is the*

Great Eagle?" she wondered, half murmuring to herself.

Fresh dread rose in her heart. The storm was coming too fast. Rolling, twisting and hurdling dust and debris high into the air, the storm roared nearer and nearer, aimed straight for her. She was still quite a distance from the mountain's cave, so, seeing a large oak tree, she headed for that instead.

As the tempest rose up against its target, she was certain she would not make it to cover. It was sure to take her out. Frantically, she crouched low to the ground, making herself as small as she could. At the last second, she ducked beneath it. Bolting back to her feet, she physically hurled it off her arms with the weight of her body. Over her head and onto the ground behind her, it flew, landing with a jarring thud. Groaning and seething, the storm revealed itself to be not just a storm, but something more sinister.

As Beloved made a dash for cover once again, she did a doubletake as it rose to its feet. In an instant, she understood this foe was none other than Jezebel.

It had been made clear she desired Beloved's death and, taking advantage of her slumber, had tried to kill her. But something had awoken the prophet just in time. Now, seeing what was really after her, she turned to face her adversary.

Jezebel grabbed her arm, twisting it violently. *"If you think I will let you get away with treating me like that, you are crazy."*

"It was you who came after me!" Beloved retorted.

Jezebel refused to recognize her and continued, *"I will destroy you. I will accuse you and they will believe me. Because I hate the prophets and I know you've been at the Great Eagle's nest. You will see what I can do..."*

"YOU ARE A LIAR!" Beloved screamed back with such authority that it made Jezebel step back a bit.

Clearly, Jezebel was attempting to distinguish if she had anything to fear from this little nothing, as she thought of her. Limiting her fury slightly, she changed her posture. *"I will make everyone hate you. Your name will be on everyone's tongue. I will pulverize your calling and make you a laughing stock! You should not have treated me like that!"*

"Well, I'm going to tell everyone the truth about you! You came after me!" Beloved tried to reason with her.

Throwing her head back and laughing, suddenly two smaller demons emerged from inside Jezebel - one was deception, the other death. In an instant, they went after Beloved. With them came horrendous fear that took her breath away. Struggling to shake them off, she twisted and screamed out in pain as one went after her heart with its talons. Dropping her to the ground, they sent waves of panic through her and thoughts of death filled her mind.

"God, help me!" she cried.

An old memory flooded back of when she was eight years old and her mother had taken her to visit an old prophetess. *"She will be the Lord's messenger to the North, South, East and West..."* her words resonated in her mind.

"I will live and not die and declare the works of the Lord!" (Psalm 118:17) she screamed as death's grip tightened around her throat.

Falling back from the impact of the Scripture, deception doubled its force and came at her again. So, Beloved continued to yell out the Word of God, *"I will not be afraid of the terror by night, nor of the arrow that flies by day"* (Psalm 91:5) *"because Great is He Who is in me than He who is in the world!"* (1 John 4:4).

Jezebel closed her eyes and pursed her lips. Driven to near madness by Scripture, she threw her head back and screamed out a fire of accusation, adding to the dust cloud of words surrounding her. Suddenly, Jezebel vomited out venom at Beloved and, just like the two demonic creatures, there were now two new Jezebels coming at her from the storm.

The first new Jezebel had a smile that made her look dumb, but she was as cunning as a knife in your back. Trying to give the impression of a deep-thinker, the second had a permanently wrinkled brow but found only the faults of others to use as weapons against them.

The smiling one stepped forward first and tried to seem calm. *"I'm just here to help you, Beloved. You need my help. We are the true prophets and we want you to join us. Come away from the false and join us. We want to be your friends. I'm seeing that God wants you to join us and you will have a big calling, Beloved."* You could see the whites in her eyes as they rolled back into her head, while her face wrinkled and twisted as if something inside her was struggling for control.

"Nothing would by any means induce me to have anything to do with you!" Beloved yelled back,

trying to seem in control, as her shock was beginning to turn to dread. *"You are as deceived as the day is long!"*

Now, it was the second Jezebel's turn. *"There's something really wrong with you, Beloved... something reeaalllyyy wrong with you. You will never fulfill your calling until you fiiixxx yourself. Let me pray for you; I can fixxx youu,"* she spoke with her wrinkled brow, acting as if she were seeing something deep inside Beloved that needed to be fixed. Repeating herself over and over, it seemed she could say nothing more than that same turn of phrase.

Realizing they were failing to convince Beloved, they began to rotate their hands in twisted motions, pretending to do miracles like Simon in the Bible. As they did, the demons from the dust storm snapped to attention. They came at Beloved and attempted to push her down. Pretending to go into trances, the Jezebels made themselves look ridiculous.

While smaller demons aided them as they made a show of their counterfeit powers, working miracles through subterfuge, they were simply oblivious to their tragically absurd behavior. Seeing their outlandish parlor tricks, her fright was replaced by indignation, as they lashed out in a war of words against her soul.

Finally, Beloved could stand their pathetic play-acting no longer. *"Just stop!"* she screamed. *"Stop it! Do you really think I am that stupid! Though you only pretend, I actually do hear from God! Do you not think that should make you fearful at all? God is real and His friendship with the true prophets is also real. Do you not think at all that He will punish you for pretending to be prophetic while operating with demons instead of the Holy Presence of God? You should be ashamed! And you should be afraid of what God will do to punish you. Do you have no fear of God at all? You are simply lost and blinded by your own self-importance. You think you see when you don't. God help you!"*

All at once, it all disappeared. The dust storm, their accusations, demons and Jezebels were gone and in their place was the Great Eagle. He was holding up a scroll that possessed two simple words: THE END.

Beloved fell to the ground and cried like she had never cried in her life as her body heaved with sobs of gratitude. Weary and relieved, she was covered in dust and sweat as the angels came to minister to her. Father's Presence washed over her like a bath in sea water. She let her body relax and her mind was shown a lovely scene of her heavenly home again. Peacefully, gently, expectantly, Beloved was met by the Spirit of the Lord, who carried her through the many layers of Earth's atmosphere, up into the expanse of space. Stationed at varying intervals in the heavens, she saw majestic angelic sentinels standing guard at their posts. Closer and closer to heaven, they ascended until they broke through to heaven's throne room.

Instantly, Beloved's eyes met the eyes of Jesus. Standing near Father's throne, all else stood still except Him. Her heartbeat rose above all her other senses, for, though He was as she had always seen Him, it was as though a mighty wind had overtaken Him and a powerful storm emanated from His person.

Although visibly heavy, His robes blew out from around Him and His tremendously long train wafted in all directions. Blending into the clouds of the tangible Presence that hovered above the crystalline surface of the room, it spread out like water converging with a river.

With earnest joy, Jesus motioned with His hand for her to come closer to the throne.

Captivated by the rolling waves of the Presence, which hovered as swirls of clouds all throughout the throne-room like a living being, she reached out to touch them and was met with peace and serenity. A giant bowl of liquid gold was poured into the clouds of the Spirit from behind the throne and instantly caught up into the waves as it flowed throughout them.

Finally, Beloved saw a most beautiful woman entering. With stateliness and tranquility, she moved gracefully toward the throne. With a crown of gold on her head, she possessed long, dark, thickly braided hair, adorned with dainty, precious flowers. Dressed in splendid robes, she was clothed in layers of white chiffon and wore a thinly interwoven golden sash around her waist. Beloved perceived her to be the church, the bride of Lord Jesus.

As the bowl of gold was delivered to the woman, she reached out and took it into her hands. Lifting it above her head, she poured it over herself. Finally, she took it to her mouth and began to drink. A sorrowful wince of pain rushed across her face. She clutched her stomach and bent over in pain. Instantly, several similarly dressed women surrounded her.

As if it were a magnificent, well-rehearsed dance, they moved into their intended places and comforted her as if she were in labor. Knowing just what to do, the ladies removed her crown and robes. They even cut away her long hair. Keenly, Beloved searched her, expecting her to appear less attractive. Instead, she was instantaneously engulfed by a glorious cloud of gold and amber fire. She appeared almost inhuman, yet was clearly a woman glorious to behold. She was a church consumed with revival fire!

Wrapped in a mighty tempest of wind, Jesus moved from His position by the Father for the first time. Tenderly, He approached the woman transformed into glory-flame and drew near to comfort her. As all eyes in the throne-room watched. He swathed her in His beautiful robe, proceeding to embrace her in His arms. Drawing back, He removed His crown and placed it upon her head, then placed His forehead against hers.

For some time, they stood in this way - an embrace of wind and fire. It looked like how she imagined Pentecost!

After witnessing this moving ceremony, Jesus finally spoke to Beloved. *"What seems like destruction brings life and becomes our greatest moment. The answer to prayers prayed from millions of saints over hundreds of years will emerge in the days ahead, more glorious than any could imagine. Truly, the church's greatest hour has finally arrived as she surrenders the burdens of her heart to a loving God. My church has a destiny, and I will not relent until My bride returns to love me afresh and anew, surrendering to Me as her One True Love.*

"Father holds the world in His hands and only in surrendered trust can the church embrace its calling. Turning her eyes away from all else and returning to My love, she will be consumed by the glory of Heaven's realm. My bride will be changed - transformed as a woman in labor, giving birth once again to eternity's outpouring and heaven's victorious invasion of Earth. As a church consumed by heaven's fire, I will hold her and embrace her with My Mighty Rushing Wind.

"Indeed, by Holy Spirit's power, My bride is about to give birth as it was prophesied over 100 years ago. All the past glorious outpourings of Holy Presence will pale in comparison to the fire He will impart in this hour.

"For two-thousand years, My church has struggled to recapture the inexhaustible joy and

freedom the early church experienced. The reformers fought for twelve-hundred years to restore My church to Me, and, in less than five-hundred years, many of My children have lost sight of what was done for them and the terrible price it cost. Trying to attain the fruit of the Spirit while kicking out Holy Spirit, they replaced it with empty words, and false prophets. They want to control My Power! Beloved, the reformation is not over and My bride must throw off the false bride and seek Me again or it will consume them.

"Ready or not, Holy Spirit is coming and He is fire and storm unlike the world has ever known. As a church, you've labored under the spirit of Jezebel and tried to work within the confines of control and manipulation. Truly, My prophets are subjected to relentless attacks. Yet, revival fires are coming! I'm sending My friends and have imbued them with My power. They will burn off the bands of slavery that have kept My bride from returning to Me.

"Seek Me again, seek My kingdom, and righteousness will cover you. Return and surrender!

"Beloved, pray with Me." He held her in His arms and, closing His eyes, spoke, *"Dearest Father, together, we seek Your face and want desperately for Your glory to be poured out on the world.*

Deliver them from Jezebel's harassment, and bind them to Your will. Do with them as You would. Help them to love You and worship You as You deserve."

9

Jehu

LORD JESUS HAD previously handed Beloved a piece of parchment and pen to take down His words. While she knelt at His feet, He concluded His instruction and turned to kiss her head. Grabbing her hand, He raised her to her feet and presented her to a tremendous crowd of people who'd been listening to His discourse nearby.

Speaking to the company, He stretched out His hand toward them and said, *"My beautiful Beloved!"*

Standing to their feet, they applauded in profound celebration that turned into joyous worship for Lord Jesus. Jumping for joy, they rejoiced, for the moment they'd anticipated had come. Their happiness was so uproarious it was even felt on Earth as the arrival of this special hour had come. Finally, it was time to release and do all which the earth would feel, as the coming impact of heaven upon the earth would be felt for all eternity.

"I honor you, Beloved. The revelations I've given you of Who I am are an honor given and a balm to heal your heart of all life's traumas," Lord Jesus began.

"Indeed, there is more to Me than what you've known, for I and My church have been maligned in the past and it is My joy and privilege that you should know Me and speak for Me. For, many are plagued with worry for the future, but I say, 'Come to Me all who are weary and heavy laden and find genuine rest in Me.' I will give them rest. I will give them peace. Rest from their toil, rest from fear, from anger, hatred and offense. And I will restore to them the fruit of love, joy, peace, patience, and kindness."

Turning from Beloved to the crowd, He continued His admonition: *"Joy is coming, My friends!"* They shouted their response of joyous exuberance. *"You will feel and see a massive wave of My Presence penetrating Earth's atmosphere. It will push back the darkness and release a hunger for holiness to My Father's children. Those who turn to Me will be freed from deception, for I'm releasing a wave of repentance. It will open their eyes and they will feel the shame they need to feel for sin. Then, I will restore them.*

"Go now and receive your victory in My name." He raised out His hands to bless His heavenly army who'd stood front and center before Him in anticipation. *"You will liberate My church, freeing them from much of the enemy's power. Receive your victory in My name. By My Word, I have decreed it and, by My Word, I will uphold it. Light the way! The cities of the earth are yours to liberate from the kingdom of darkness. 'Liberate the kingdoms of Earth,' will be your battle cry. Pursue the lost and strengthen the weary, cripple the enemy's power to deceive. Armies of Heaven, you represent Me in this fight. Be swift, sure and true. You will be victorious over your enemy."*

Repeatedly in this way, He blessed the various battalions of His army with the point of His scepter, giving them direction and instruction for their battle. Every soldier had a circular shield that spun from a point in the middle. It was surrounded with dart-like weapons attached to the turning edge, each one armed with conviction.

Lord Jesus explained, *"Holy Spirit enjoys bringing conviction to the hearts of men, for the God of War is warring against the Babylonian deception flooding the earth. My brothers and sisters have been praying for faith, strength and power but are afraid of My answer. I need you to help them receive Holy Spirit and bring them the answer to their prayers!"*

The heavenly celebration went on for quite some time, continuing even after Beloved had reentered Earth's realm. Yet, she longed for a quiet place of her own and had grown fond of the little cabin on the forsaken side of Father's mountain. Just as the thought transpired in her mind, she was returned to it again.

Since the night of the three horses, she felt close to the Father in this old shack on the barren side of His mountain. With only a coarsely made desk, bed and a few other necessities, it felt like home for some reason. She received keen revelation while here and, remembering Great Eagle's nest, she wondered if Father had intended this little cabin to be hers.

Yet, after returning to the earth's realm, Beloved couldn't stop thinking of the harvest. It was all heaven talked about. Something had been planted inside of her. Suddenly, she remembered the Bible story of Cain, who was driven by jealousy to murder his brother, Abel, and how it had all taken place during the harvest.

"Of course," she mumbled to herself, *"this must have greatly limited their ability to bring in their crops."* Suddenly, Beloved felt ill-at-ease for the sake of Earth's harvest at hand and realized, *the enemy would try to hinder their harvesting through strife, offense and jealousy, causing them to hate each other and limit the souls redeemed.* (Genesis 4:3-12)

She had felt in her spirit an unsettling anger growing in Earth's atmosphere, and suddenly understood what was happening. This anger was, indeed, directed at those who were currently winning the lost to Christ. *Will it try to threaten the harvest,* she wondered. *Is jealousy at work again?*

"Yes!" She grabbed at her throat and gasped. *"This is the enemy's plan of attack. He will try to delay or even stop many from believing in Lord Jesus. A vicious plan!"* she exclaimed as she pounded her first into the palm of her hand. *"Just like Cain killed Abel. And even if we don't murder our brother or sister, slander will do a great deal of damage!"*

Beloved groaned as she thought of all the countless babes in the Lord who might listen to the slander and be turned away from hearing about their Savior. Listening to the gossip and rage of deceived believers, they would be poisoned against the only one Who could save them.

"We've got to pray for the harvest. Aren't we commanded to pray for the harvest. In the Bible… somewhere?" She looked up to heaven, praying, *"Now is the time to activate the intercessors, Father, and fight for the harvest. Help us watch for the enemy and guard our hearts to keep us from falling into Satan's schemes that would limit us in receiving our harvest."*

"Father, You promised us in Your Word the souls of men as our inheritance!" She pointed to the heavens, *"Watch and stand guard over the harvest, Father, for our adversary, the devil, 'prowls around like a roaring lion, looking to devour us' (1 Peter 5:8). Build Your walls of righteousness around us and keep that thief at bay! Papa! Give us our rightful inheritance as Your sons and daughters! In Jesus' name!"*

All alone in a forlorn cabin on the barren side of God's mountain, Beloved was naturally surprised when she suddenly, pulled from her intercession, heard someone calling out for her.

"Beloved!"

Mystified, she peered out of the half-hung door of the cabin to find a man she'd never met come racing up to meet her.

"Are you Beloved?" he shouted.

"Yes?" she answered sheepishly.

"Hellooooo!" Calling back to her was a frothy man, who was as lively as anyone she'd ever met.

"What's wrong with everybody?" he asked, acting as though they were familiar with one another and in the course of a conversation. *"I keep asking everyone I've met,"* he continued as he charged up to the porch of the old cabin to meet her, *"and no one seems to know anything!"*

"It seems the very least they would do is to send me to you, and you are none too easy to find. And this place! My Heavens! What a place. It looks like God just put it up yesterday." He gave out a hearty laugh and was quite pleased with himself. *"Alright, missy! What are we going to do about it? What are we going to do, that's what I've been asking ya?"* He barked at her like he was accustomed to being the boss.

Simply baffled, Beloved could barely get a word in to ask him what he was talking about. Wide-eyed, she finally managed to slip in, *"Sir, I am very sorry, but I really don't understand you. What is it you are having trouble with?"*

Barely giving her enough time to finish, he jumped in again, *"Well, finding you, for one thing - that was a problem. What is this place? What kinda crazy person would be found in a place like this, that's what I want to know?!"* He finally paused to glare down at her.

"I guess you want a reply, don't you?" she answered.

"That's what I'm aiming at, li'l miss."

Beloved stalled to pull her reasoning together. She didn't quite understand what drew her to this place. Though it was probably the authentic aspects of the surroundings, she hadn't really stopped to think about it. *"I guess I just really like it, sir…"*

Cutting her off, he began again, *"What is wrong with everyone, Beloved? Wait, that's your name, right? That's what they told me down yonder."*

"Yes!" She snuck in a reply with a cheeky grin. *"What's yours?"*

"What's wrong with everybody?" He continued. *"Huh?"* He stopped to redirect his energy. *"Oh,*

that's right! Introductions are in order. Forgive me, little one." He stuck out his hand to shake hers and added, *"My name is Jehu!"*

"Ahhhh," Beloved thought to herself, *"he is the one I've heard about."*

"Why doesn't someone do something about it?" he inquired once again, pacing back and forth in the dirt while Beloved stood in the doorway of the cabin.

"Do something about what?" she asked. *"Nice to meet you, by the by."*

"Why, Jezebel, of course! He stopped abruptly and stared at her petulantly. *"I've been told of her attack against you. Can't stand that demon!"*

With that, Beloved left the door of the cabin and planted herself on the steps of the porch. She was finally interested in this man. Ready to listen and wanting to know more, she asked, *"What will you do about her?"*

"Beloved, I don't really know yet. I'm not the type of person to 'make plans,' as they say," he said. *"I just flow..."* He made a river motion with his hand. *"What I do know is those Jezebel's will keep popping up until they're dealt with!"*

This was music to Beloved's ears and an answer to her prayers. *"Thank you, Lord Jesus,"* she said as she looked to the Lord. *"Finally, someone who will teach me to conquer that old crone!"*

"From what I've seen, she's an out and out bully and she cannot be tolerated. You can't make a purse out of a sow's ear, is what I'm saying. You can't be friends with her, because she'll take your friendship and use it against you. She doesn't know how to be a friend. So, you give her your honest-to-goodness friendship and she'll give you a hefty stab in the back in thanks. What she wants isn't friendship. She wants control, and she'll worm it out of you one way or another. She's not a prophet either. Her 'prophecies,'" he said while making quotation marks with his fingers, all the while snarling out the side of his face, *"they are just lies that come with an agenda. People think one prophecy is as good as another, but hers will kill ya! Naw, you can't hear from God through a Jezebel. He don't talk to them! They are as fake as the day is long!"*

"That's what I said!" Beloved remarked, laughing as he continued.

"Elijah was afraid of her and it almost drove him mad. You can't be afraid of Jezebel. That's her way. She gains power over you by making you fearful of her. That's why," he laughed out loud,

"that's why, Beloved, you need someone crazy... like me!" He bellowed out a hefty laugh, entirely amused with himself.

This man is truly uncompromised, she realized, *and could absolutely care less what anyone thinks of him. In fact,* she chuckled to herself, *I think he enjoys offending people. This is his calling...* Her eyes were opening now. *"His gifting!"* she muttered. *The Spirit of the Lord is upon him, calling out for the justice of God! He must have been sent by Lord Jesus, for what does he have to gain by helping me?* She sensed Holy Spirit's input in these thoughts.

In the meantime, he went on, *"People let that woman, Jezebel, and her pathetic husband get away with murder, until Elijah just had enough of them both and then the Lord sent me in."* He laughed heartily. *"That was sure a fun day!"*

Beloved couldn't help liking Jehu, and admired his forthright manner.

"Yep, in my day, we wasted no time in dealing with her. She'd gotten away with destroying people's lives for so long. She can't stand you genuine prophets, on account of her having accumulated so many false ones to do her bidding - she's got quite a collection now! So many people fall for these phonies because they don't know the Scriptures, I

guess. *If they knew their Scriptures, they'd know she's a pathological liar!"*

Hearing him talk made her feel better about the effects of Jezebel's attack against her. *"Yeah, that's what she did. She lied so well. I started to believe her accusations against me, even though I clearly know the truth.*

"She hates the Lord's prophets because they speak for Him. As long as there's even one voice speaking for the Lord, she'll have a harder time making people believe her lyin' prophets. As long as there is a Jeremiah, people don't fall for the Hananiahs. But it ain't always fun for the Jeremiahs, let me tell you. What they got to say ain't as nice. People like chocolate more than vinegar. But the way I figure it, we need the Lord Jesus and no matter what He's got to say, it's good. 'Cause we're His church and He'll make us what He needs us to be, no matter what. There's always a little rough with the smooth, you know, and if they're saying there ain't, then it's probably one of them Jezebel-prophets. But the Lord says it will be worth it.

"And even you, Beloved. This battle is for you."

Suddenly, wide-eyed again, she asked, *"How so?"*

"Well, you've just been with the Great Eagle, haven't you?" Not waiting for an answer, he continued, *"Well, that's it. She smells blood in the water... her blood. And she knows if she can get you at the beginning when you don't know as much, she can either corrupt ya or kill ya. She'll try the first one first. But after that, it's a battle for her survival, because you're a threat to her way of life, Beloved.*

"It's like me - I was anointed by God to destroy her whole family, because God wanted to avenge the murder of His prophets and everyone she and her husband killed. So, this woman who'd seemed invincible and unstoppable, the 'tyrant of Israel,' an overwhelming intimidating figure that everyone was so afraid of, I killed just like that. Yet, surely, you'd think, since she was seemingly so 'all-powerful' it would be difficult to kill her, right? But I figure the Lord had had enough and it was the deaths of the prophets that brought about her death and my calling was to just finish it off. The Lord takes it personal when His prophets are attacked. After years of Jezebel's tyranny, she could no longer hurt anyone. She assumed she was invincible and yet, when God decided the time had come for her destruction, she was gone - simply and absolutely. Just like that... she was gone.

"Just like you, Beloved. He saw it all and their attack against you hurt Him deeply. He said, 'It's time for Justice!' She came at you until you wanted to hide, isn't that right?"

Beloved nodded in agreement.

"She makes you want to come out here in the wilderness and hide in this old dried out cabin of yours until it takes someone like me, who's real determined to find you. I am a reformer - probably one of the first - and I can't stand injustice. I take no prisoners. Lord Jesus has mercy, that's His job. But, me? I just wanna get er done." He smiled at Beloved and winked. *"Well, there's no sense waiting or worrying. Let's just get at it..."*

He stopped for a minute and said, *"But there's a lotta good to say about her, too."*

Beloved looked shocked by this, but he ignored her as he explained himself.

"When Jezebel attacks, it shows you your weakness and, instead of tearing you up, God makes sure it draws you closer to Him and it purifies you instead. True love is honest first of all and courageous secondly. Conviction is love; tolerating sin is hate."

"That's what I wondered," Beloved answered. *"'Why are they attacking me?' Then I realized it*

must not be for what I've done in the past, but what I will do in the future."

"You got it!" Jehu answered with satisfaction.

"I do feel God has drawn me closer to Him through her attacks," she continued. *"He actually commissioned me right after that. I thought to myself, after I recovered a little bit that, if there are fakers like her in the mission fields, maybe God really does need me. And maybe I wasn't so ill-equipped for His service after all. It seemed the more she attacked me, the greater my confidence grew and the more I learned about her, and how to fight her. I learned not to fear, but to fear being disobedient to God alone. He's the one in control - not her!"*

Jehu threw his head back in a bout of laughter. He'd been watching her passion come alive the longer she talked about it. It pleased him to see it. *"Whoooopeee!"* He shouted as he threw his hat in the air.

"That's it, Beloved! He smiled. *When you throw her out a window, it feels pretty good!"*

He knew she was ready then. He'd kept talking until he knew her heart was right and she had learned what God wanted her to realize at last. Jehu raised his hands to his mouth and cupped them around it to magnify his yell. Calling up to heaven, he cried out for the Hounds of Heaven to be unleashed. Instantly, they were in the clouds above. Escorted by the angelic, they dove down to where the two of them stood.

"That was sure quick!" Jehu remarked. *"They must've been ready to go!"* He laughed.

Beloved was astonished by the incredible, ferocious beasts who seemed quite familiar with Jehu. He greeted them as friends, but also with the respect owed a fellow warrior. Without much conversation between them, they were given their orders. As he pointed to her and then beyond, they set out.

Watching readily, Beloved couldn't help expecting more to happen, but it seemed he had completed his mission.

"That's it?" she asked, confused but not wanting to appear so.

"Well," he said, much more relaxed than before, *"once you get it, Beloved, and you are ready to be done with her oppression and wanna throw her out the window, it's pretty much down-hill climbing from there. Firstly, the work is done in you and once you decide not to tolerate her anymore, God takes care of the rest. Don't you worry a bit about it, lil*

missy. You ain't the same as you were before and God's gonna make her pay for hurting you. It will be worth it." He winked at her as he lifted his hat, and nodded a farewell, exiting as briskly as he'd arrived.

For the first time, Beloved felt her eyes were really opened to who she truly was, who her Father was and how the enemy had taken advantage of her. Moving swiftly to her aid, Lord Jesus had cast out those who would be her captors and tormentors. He set her on the throne He'd prepared for her, convincing her of the beauty she alone possessed and of the kingdom she must fight to save. The harvest was great and the workers few, indeed. Looking toward the kingdom of heaven, she cried out, knowing He was there to hear her, *"I am ready Lord!"*

10

HOUSE OF PRAYER

AFTER EVERYTHING BELOVED had gone through, she'd thought she had reached the end of what she could endure and just wanted to hide from the world. However, after one afternoon with Jehu, she felt more like herself or, truly, more than herself. Indeed, she was the person she'd long wished to be.

At last, she felt like she wanted to be with other believers, to fellowship with them in the Lord's house. Of all the things she'd promised herself, the most important was she would live to please her Savior, not caring or being moved by the opinions of others. It was manipulation that pressed her heart to the brink of cruelty and thought in the past it would be her greatest enemy for the rest of her life, never again would she tolerate those who would have her turn herself inside-out just to please them.

Walking toward the House of Prayer, she'd been invited to meet up with a group of believers there she'd only heard about. Although she had been made aware of her weaknesses, she had also received so much confidence and strength from her journeys, and she knew she couldn't let fear hold her back from the appointment.

On entering the small patchwork building, she was surprised to see it packed with people filling every corner. Beloved was hit by the expectancy that filled the room as the happy people fervently contended for an outpouring of Holy Spirit to manifest in their midst. Most of those there were young or middle aged, except for an old man sitting in a rocking chair surrounded by people. On seeing her, the room burst into jubilant greetings, and she was warmed by their celebratory welcome. She was happy she had joined them.

After meeting all those who'd so anxiously waited for her arrival, Beloved was drawn, even compelled, to meet the older man in the rocker. It was clear he had waited for her to notice him as well.

"Beloved," he began, reaching to take her hand in his, *"many of my generation have been waiting for an outpouring of God's Presence in the world. Now, they are older and have begun to lose faith. Please, tell them they will see the movement of the Spirit they've waited for. Tell them they will, indeed, see it."* He seemed emphatic and relieved to finally convey his message to her and she was grateful to have received it.

As she turned to take in the rest of those in the room, she realized a small band of older believers had followed her into the building. Suddenly, as the two generations merged, the Glory of God fell in the place! Like a burst of lightning, the glory of heaven hit the room and it erupted with intense, overwhelming joy!

There were few words to describe what it felt like. It was as though an explosion from heaven hit them. All at once, they started to roar in song,

'THERE'S NO GOD LIKE JEHOVAH!' Their worship mushroomed into a visible cloud and brought an even greater triumph of concentration of rejoicing. Miracles began to break out as supernatural phenomenons manifested all over them that they could neither explain nor contain!

A Voice from the cloud began to speak, *"You will see My hand in your midst! You will see My Glory poured out on the earth! You will see the promises made to you fulfilled! What your generation has been watching and praying for will come to pass. You will experience the coming renewal of My Presence in your land!"*

The Voice continued, *"I will renew your youth and restore your vigor as you seek My face and spread the joy of My coming. I will reach down My hand and give you the generations through this movement. Many who My church thought were unreachable will be given to you. This you will see so My name will be praised in all the earth! From all walks of life, they will turn to Me, and you will have no doubt that I am doing this – these who I give you will be absolutely MINE! They will walk with Me like the prophets of old and will hear My voice and speak what I tell them to speak. You must listen and learn, for there is something I want to show you through their lives. Love them as you have loved Me and you will receive an overwhelming impartation of My Spirit that will spread worldwide.*

"Wise ones! I have kept you for this hour. You've been steadfast and faithful to believe in Me. Even though some of your generation have fallen, you have remained with Me and believed in Me. I will reward you for your trust. I have loved you and will show others how much you are valued and loved by Me. You will be rewarded in this life and the next. I speak through you and I will show the world you are Mine. Trust Me in this hour like you've never trusted before. Stand close to Me, for I have not left your side. You will be made into an iron tower of glory that many will seek as refuge in the coming days. Stand firm!

"For a time and for a season, I have allowed darkness to run rampant. Even they have been surprised by how much they've been able to accomplish. Yet, I have allowed this. I am preparing My bride and I am revealing the hearts of My people. And I will turn the chaos over and reveal My glory to the nations.

"Remember, I come in whispers, not in screams, but I will roar over the nations and shake

mountains. Have you been impressed by mountains? Truly, I am impressed by My friends!"

The room erupted with praise, thanksgiving and a resounding *"YES! What we've waited for we will surely see! Praise Lord Jesus, the Lord of hosts!"* Their praise went on for many hours as they continued to celebrate Father's wonderful words to them.

Much later, after the room quieted down, they conversed about all the Father had said to them, Beloved shared a recent vision. *"By the Spirit, I saw a great army held in reserve until this hour. At last, they are being released by Father. I saw them as they were set to task for the Lord and burst forth with such vigor and joy that it made me cry with delight to see them. They rode on horses, dressed in all the plume and regalia of a most valiant army. I saw the faces of these warriors and they were not young by human standards, yet they were full of more life than they'd had in their twenties and thirties, only now they were filled with wisdom that would saturate the earth and bring peace to the younger warriors.*

"As I watched gleefully this great army emerge ready for battle, I saw they were unaware of a tremendous cobra that had risen up behind them. I

felt sure it would destroy them all in one strike of its enormous head.

"Yet, just as surely as I saw the cobra, I saw directly behind it another being that was even larger. Just as unexpected, a Great Lion appeared behind the snake. And as the snake readied itself to strike against the warriors, the Lion rose against the cobra. In one movement, it gobbled up the snake. Meanwhile, the warriors were not even aware they had been in danger!

"So it will be with this generation," she spoke out boldly. *"You will ride to battle with euphoric joy and the enemy will be swallowed up behind you. For, the Lord says, 'I will be faithful to My ANNAS and My SIMEONS. What I have promised to them, they will see and they will protect the movement of My hand and will bring greatly needed help to My children! Fear nothing. This is the hour to rejoice - the hour you've long awaited! It is yours, My wise ones. Take it and enjoy the day I have given to you! Arise and take back this land. Take back the generations and give them to Me, for I am ready to receive them! I will make your enemies a footstool for you!'"*

As all of them rejoiced in what Beloved shared, a young man named Raleigh rose up and addressed the room, *"Our Lord has promised a day of judgment for the arrogant evildoer, a day that will leave no 'root or branch,' (Malachi 4:1). In that glorious day, we will behold our Lord and Savior, Jesus of Nazareth, and we will understand a level of joy that is inconceivable to us now. He is preparing for that day! In that day, He will send Elijah to - 'turn the hearts of the fathers to their children, and the hearts of the children to their fathers,' (Malachi 4:6) or our God will 'strike the land with a curse.'"*

Beloved felt a hand on her arm and, in turning to answer it, she saw the old man who'd left his rocker. He was crying and wanted to address the room, *"Friends, we've cried from the depths of our hearts for the intervening hand of a merciful God, Who even now will forgive our sins as we turn to Him. If we humbly pray and seek the face of God, turn away from the sins of the world and church, and live only for Him, He will hear us from heaven and graciously stave off the curse on our nation,"* (1 Chronicles 7:14).

As he spoke in earnest a sincere hush fell over the people, intercession began to pour from the group, *"Father,"* they spoke in one accord, *"unite the generations. Holy Spirit, manifest in us as you did in the days of Elijah. Merge hearts together and make us one holy vessel to receive Your Holy Spirit once again! In Jesus' name!"*

As the intercessors prayed in the spirit, the angelic were gathered too. One of their rank came and requested Beloved's presence in their meeting. She followed him into another part of the house, and as they rounded the corner, she began to hear a song of praise unlike what she'd ever heard before. It was incredible and unearthly as it rang:

Jesus is the Cornerstone,
Jesus is the Cornerstone!
Victory lies in the Cornerstone,
give Him glory and honor.
Victory lies in the Cornerstone!
All hail Jesus the Cornerstone.
Praise His name, most glorious name.
Jesus, our Cornerstone!

"This is so beautiful!" she cried. *"How lovely to hear you praise Jesus! Thank you so much for showing me this. Please tell me, what does this mean? The Cornerstone is, indeed, the answer, but what do we need to do? Tell me, please, dear friend!"* She felt certain this was the answer they'd been contending for.

"Beloved," the angel began, *"to give you a quick lesson of the Cornerstone, I would be ever so grateful if you would oblige me by letting me share a story with you. Would that please you, Beloved?"*

"Of course," she nodded excitedly.

"Well," he answered, *"there was a family who lived on a farm in the country. Unfortunately, this farm was near where some who operate in the dark arts lived as well. As time passed, the family was cursed relentlessly by their neighbors. They were being spiritually bullied and had no way of understanding what was truly happening to them or how to stop it. Over time, the father of the family began to drink heavily and would become violent. Incredible self-hatred filled him with rage that ate away at his soul, causing him to take it out on his family.*

"One day, the man beat his wife until her back was broken and she was paralyzed. The violence that took hold of the family turned dark and disturbing. Sadly, the sons transferred their hostility against their younger sister in perverse acts. With their family falling apart, eventually the farm was put up for sale.

"Purchased by another family, the spirits collided with them as well. Much pain tried to

invade this new family. Self-hatred continued to rain down and drew them all to their breaking point, but this family was a praying family. One night while praying, they were led to call out to God for the Cornerstone to save them, and wash the sin and trauma away. Again and again, they entreated the Lord to come and make things new - to cleanse the land with the precious blood of the Lamb.

"Fighting back long and hard, they defended themselves against the onslaught of witchcraft trying to destroy them. Finally, one day, four white doves flew into the farm as though they were measuring it for size. By and by, they came once more to the little farm in the country and in their beaks they each held fast to a piece of cloth that held a giant stone. The stone they carried was the same size as the property and as they worked to position it just right, they let it drop on the farm.

"Filling every inch of their farm, all that had happened in the past was buried beneath it, stamping it out permanently and renewing the land. Lo, all was made new again. The past was gone and the trauma that occurred there was transformed to joy. A new foundation was laid and the sins of men were canceled out. Behold, all was made brand new - a new Foundation was lain.

"Do you understand what I'm saying, Beloved?" he asked.

"If you don't mind, I would like you to explain it to me," she answered.

"Shame is spiritually corrosive to the human soul and as sin takes hold, so does self-hatred. It opens the door to the demonic realm to come and take possession. Even though the new family prayed, the protection was hard won because the door to self-hatred was established there. It's the new beginning brought by Lord Jesus, our blessed Cornerstone that will cancel out all established evil used against us. All demonic obligation no longer exists as the Stone buries all sin and crushes the past, ushering in a new season that can be anything you dream of. It's a new season, Beloved. Shame held sin in place, but the Cornerstone renews your hope and your new season is at hand!"

Beloved replied, *"This should change everything! Thank you so much for telling me. How wonderful I feel! This will bring such hope to so many. We'll be returning soon to the fields of grace and I am thrilled to share about the Cornerstone! Praise God for the Cornerstone! Indeed, Cornerstone changes everything."*

"That's why Elohim wanted us to share it with you, so that you could, in turn, share it with those in need. But let me show you one more thing." Turning back to the side of the room, he showed her a record player and on it was one album that played the same song the angels were singing, *"Jesus is the Cornerstone!"*

She looked up at him quizzically.

As he smiled back at her, he said. *"The Cornerstone wants you to meet Him, Beloved. You will find Him in the fields of grace!"*

11

MOUNTAIN OF SOULS

BUSY WORKING IN the heat of the day, Beloved never minded the labor she sowed into the fields of grace, no matter how difficult. Lord Jesus had asked her to wait for Him there and she was enjoying the bright sunshine as she did. This day, while reaping, she noticed a dear woman in the fields trying to catch her eye. She waved at Beloved as though she knew her.

"Beloved!" she called excitedly for her to come.

Lit up from the inside, she was very beautiful with long, dark-brown hair tied up in a bun. Thrilled, Beloved recognized her as Maria Woodworth-Etter, a great woman evangelist. At the turn of the twentieth century, many were healed and led to the saving knowledge of Lord Jesus through her ministry. It was a great honor to meet up with her here as she called to Beloved as though they were friends.

"Beloved, there are corpses in the wheat," she said matter-of-factly.

Beloved was shocked by the woman's frankness as she showed her the bodies that appeared as little more than a mass of dirt and plant.

"They are very dead, but don't worry," she soothed. *"The wheat grows even upon the corpses."*

Beloved decided it was best just to smile and nod because she didn't have any idea what she could be talking about. And it was a good thing she took it in stride, for the woman of God showed her a great deal about the white fields of grace. Beloved soon found she liked her very much. Tying the wheat into bundles exactly as Maria had taught her, she learned all she could from this great woman of God. Beloved flew through the wheat and cut the stalks with ease until her arms were brimming, and she did not want to drop even one grain of wheat.

Seeing her struggle, Maria shouted, *"There's room in that wagon over there."* She pointed to a very large wooden wagon used communally.

As Beloved placed her wheat safely in the wagon, she was met by Lord Jesus, her wonderful Cornerstone.

"This wagon's nearly full, Beloved. Take your bundles to My wagon." He motioned to the base of an old tree on the border of the field. *"Thank you, Beloved!"* He sang while He worked in the fields. Smiling that big happy grin of His, He threw her a bag of gold.

Thinking it strange, she hollered back at Him, *"Are you paying me for the wheat?"*

Throwing His head back and giving the air a hearty laugh, he bellowed at her, *"It's to use to buy more treasure and redeem more souls!"*

She lit up with understanding, for she'd already had an idea of just what He wanted her to do. *"Just like the talents,"* (Matthew 25:14–30) she laughed to herself.

She turned back around and headed back into the wheat field alongside Ms. Etter. But after working with her for a while longer, she was surprised to suddenly see Helen. Looking up across the distance of the field, she found her working alongside the Lord. She was a favorite, old friend of hers who was part of the prophetic host. It was clear that, in her turn, she was delighted to see Beloved.

Running to embrace her, Beloved couldn't get over her astonishment in seeing her again. Meeting her was always like reconnecting with herself because she knew her so well. She soon learned that Lord Jesus had asked her to meet Him there as well. He'd said He had a special surprise for them both.

"Beloved, Father has planned that you and I will work together. Side by side, we will work to bring in the harvest." Beloved cried from the joy of all the precious gifts the Lord was giving them both.

It was a very lovely time as they embraced each other at length. Helen's hugs were like powerful chargers! But the Lord's great big arms came and grabbed Beloved and turned her to Himself. *"My Turn!"* He said as he hugged her as well. Suddenly, Jesus pulled back and roared over her as He turned from a man to a lion and then back again. She could feel the intense sound turn to fire as it hit her and filled her with life.

"The fire is meant to cleanse you of weakness and make you stronger," Helen explained. *"For you*

are still very vulnerable to the enemy. Truly, the Lord's hugs are powerful!" she laughed.

Lord Jesus then turned and motioned with His hand off in the distance and asked, "Beloved, what do you see?"

"I see a very big mountain, Lord, and its covered in snow. How beautiful..." Then, squinting, she said, Wait! What is that?" She stopped in her tracks and stared at the mountain for a while. Suddenly, she realized it was not covered in snow, but with people in white garments. The snow looked like it was waving at her, but it was thousands of people joyously greeting her.

Beloved turned to the Lord for answers. "What does it mean, Lord? Who are they?"

"They are all yours," He spoke tenderly. "I'm saving them for you to win. They are waiting for you."

Beloved was choked with emotion. She had prayed all her life that He would allow her to bring souls into the harvest. She was so overwrought with emotion that she couldn't speak for some time. Seeing her affected state, both Lord Jesus and Helen grabbed an arm to steady her and were rejoicing in their hearts. Standing in awe at the mountain before her, she was simply overcome and her dear friends were very pleased.

"Beloved, this is My delight for you," Lord Jesus reiterated. *"My compassion toward the lost is overwhelming at times. Knowing they are lost and confused like sheep without a Shepherd makes My delight in your heart all the sweeter. As I told My disciples, 'The harvest is great, but the workers are few. So, pray for the workers. Ask Me to raise up more workers who are willing to enter the fields of grace.'*

"Now is the time for My bride to awaken and activate the laborers to fight for the harvest. And, even more so, pray for them to be sober and vigilant - to watch for the enemy and guard their hearts to keep them from the snares of the enemy that would keep them from receiving.

"I have promised an inheritance; it is your destiny! Watch and stand guard over it because our adversary the devil prowls around like a roaring lion, looking for someone to devour, (1 Peter 5:8). He is seeking those he can use to steal all that belongs to Me - our rightful inheritance as God's sons and daughters."

"The battle we fight is God's war," Helen added. *"It's the battle for mankind. We are made*

victorious in Him as we battle unseen forces for the souls of men - all souls, even those who've persecuted us.

"Pray with me." She grabbed Beloved's hand and closed her eyes. *"Protect all that You've birthed in Beloved this day, Father. Make her strong in You. I declare: Beloved will be mighty in the power of Your strength. She will not stop; she will not even slow down!"*

"Father," Lord Jesus chimed in, *"I ask that you would deliver those caught in bondage. Redeem them and restore them to their rightful place in Your family. Pour out Your love on them and help them to fulfill their destiny in You."*

"Make us one," Beloved added, *"one with You and in You and may we truly become a glorious, radiant example of Your goodness and power to help others see You. Guard us against the plans of the enemy; don't let him steal our harvest, Father. And, I do declare: I will be mighty in the power of Your strength. I will not stop; I will not even slow down!"*

12

ENCOUNTERING
WARRIORS

AS LORD JESUS had planned to take Beloved back to the Father's mountain, He'd managed to procure two fine mares for their journey. Riding side by side with the Lord near the outside regions of the fields of grace, He sang a jolly little tune to Himself, *"Raise an army, prepare the way, light the torch - it's time to play!"*

Traveling through the fields of grace, Beloved saw the remnants of the armies of darkness gathering, searching in earnest for the armies of the light. The discord in the fields was heightening. It was not as peaceful as it had been and it concerned her. She knew the prophetic host was well-seasoned, but they were not yet commissioned by Lord Jesus. Their absence made her uneasy. She could see the demonic horde assembling in some places and was sure they were to blame for the unrest among the workers in the fields. They had learned to be on the look-out for invading witches, who were always seeking an advantage to overtake the laborers.

Beloved was saddened to think of the fields she loved so much under such attack, *"This truly is like a war,"* she spoke aloud without realizing.

After a pause, Lord Jesus asked, *"Are you afraid of war, Beloved?"* Without waiting for an answer, He continued, *"My warriors are not afraid to fight. They anticipate it."* He smiled at her. *"It is only through war that you obtain the spoils of war, to deliver and redeem the souls of man. This war is like no earthly battle, for we are fighting those we're trying to save, against a well-armed enemy with no natural weapons of our own. Yet..."* He paused, *"we cannot help but win.*" He smiled broadly to lighten her mood.

Bundled carefully, Beloved carried the banner she'd hoped to inspire the troops with as a gust of wind suddenly blew, nearly knocking it from her grip. The gale seemed simply unbearable and aggravated her already unsettled nerves. *"Why am I so anxious?"* she sighed.

Responding, Lord Jesus chuckled as He reasoned with her, *"Well, darlin', this battle is for nothing less than the freedom of the whole world and the eternal destination of millions of souls - no biggy! But do not fear. I have a surprise for you at Father's mountain that will alleviate your anxiousness."*

Truly, this battle was being waged by hundreds of thousands to redeem millions of souls and for the control of Christendom. Would the young reformers have the fortitude to champion for Christ as the ancient ones had, who gave nothing less than their lives? Only God knew. Beloved was confident but wanted very much to begin. *Where is my army?* her anxious thoughts questioned.

This war would be unique in the fact that the armies facing each other across the continents were distinguished only by the assumed characteristics of either the light or the darkness they served. And the followers of Christ too often mistook guile for Christlikeness.

Beloved could sense as they continued to ride in the tall growing wheat that the ferocious anger of the dark soldiers seemed to be increasing. *Would the army of light succumb to their manipulations and fall into their all-consuming breath of fury?* she worried.

She then remembered her dream about the army of fire and all they'd been through to prepare them for this hour. She reminded herself of their fearlessness and how they seemed to anticipate the enemy's wrath, yet were unaffected by it. She had great confidence in their deep-seated compassion and patience. They would not strike out in anger in the midst of even the most tangible rage. Suddenly, a smile spread across her face as she recalled their smiles. *Aaah, yes, they had the most effervescent, disarming smiles.* How she missed them.

The army of darkness seemed fierce and formidable as they were eager to exact their long-anticipated vengeance against the army of light, spitting out every repugnant, malicious curse they could muster. It was simply the most un-civil conduct she'd ever seen, but it was war, after all, and this was their weapon of choice: words.

Stopping suddenly, Lord Jesus informed, *"I think we need to leave the horses here and finish on foot. We don't want to stand out."* Securing the horses under the shade of a broad oak tree, they remained close to the edge of the field and set out to meet up with the intercessory prayer-warriors. Prepared to trek a great distance, she was surprised to find, crouched down in the grass, warriors of the light. Dressed as normal, everyday laborers in the field, they were everywhere. Hidden in plain sight, right under the noses of the army of darkness, they appeared quite innocuous and common.

"How brilliant!" She shrieked without thinking. Quieting herself, she whispered to them as she got down to their level among the wheat, *"I mean... How brilliant!"* she whispered. *"You really are the best intercessors Father has ever prepared. You are so fearless! Surrounded by thousands and thousands of the most insidious mob I've ever seen, you're waiting here as if for a surprise party."* Beloved was so excited and relieved to see them that her emotions got the better of her until a dear sister-warrior smiled at her with wide eyes, pointing

to a group of detestable demons near them. She put her finger to her lips, cautioning her to be silent.

Happy to comply, and trusting their wisdom, Beloved suddenly wondered why they were so close to the enemy. Studying them one by one, she realized they were not completely silent. They were each, in their own way, praying in hushed tones under their breath. What uncanny power seemed to be communicated in that seemingly breathless way. Undeniably, she could feel the effects of it the longer she remained with them, for they were truly changing the atmosphere.

Brilliant! she wanted to scream again. *They are wearing them down with prayer. First wrestling with the demons and disabling them, then, with stalwart love, they fight for those under the control of the power of the army of darkness.*

Still overjoyed, Beloved was elated she had encountered the warriors in action for the first time and in such a personal way. She was quite surprised by how unassuming they all were, so resolute and wise. Indeed, there seemed to be no outward signs of the power that lay in any of them. Except for their eyes, which revealed signs of an extraordinary inner strength, they seemed perfectly average. With no apparent distinguishing characteristics, the light in their eyes seemed rather familiar to her. Indeed, Father's love was in them.

Beloved heard a flood of curses unleashed against the fields of grace and the armies of light. Like dreadful bombs of dark delusion, demons used God's creation as weapons of mass destruction. Lost in the enemy's deception, they released incantations and spells like nets that flew wide against the fields. Prepared for the onslaught of demonic slime, the army of the light held firm as the craftiness of the enemy rained down upon their heads until it seemed they would be suffocated by it. Yet, like a shield, they prayed Holy Spirit's power into the atmosphere to counteract the sorcery. In a few moments, they were able to dispel the demonic declarations against them. As prayer beamed like a radiant beacon of light through the smothering gloom launched at them, it broke apart the curses with ease. Repeatedly, the light army endured the onslaught of their black arts, as incantations were released against them. Each time, enduring slander and hatred, they withstood it brilliantly.

Evermore curious, Beloved quietly asked questions of these valiant warriors. *"Why do you not all band together and display a great show of strength to make your enemies back down?"*

A woman named Donna answered first since she was the closest to her. *"In years past, there were great engagements put together by famously-named warriors, but we've not been able to form so large an assembly for some time."*

Interrupted by another barrage of curses, they were needed to refocus on intercession. But, as soon as it had past, they returned to their conversation.

"Father has told us we are more powerful than any great named warriors," David spoke up. *"As we are unknown, we are more able to hide. We are much more than we appear. Our support is vast and wide-spread. All over the earth, we are hidden in plain sight of the enemy and have tremendous effect wherever Father sends us."*

Beloved was amazed. *"Your harmonious responses are like a great dance. How did you learn to respond to it as you do?"*

"Simple survival," David answered.

"We fell in with just the wrong people and had to learn to combat their attacks against us or die," Donna added. *"Sadly, we've seen many perish because they refused to acknowledge what was attacking them."*

"They thought God was testing them," David barked.

Beloved caught Donna's eye as she nodded in agreement, *"What a laugh the enemy had when, instead of contending with the enemy's attack against them, they gave God the credit for it. That was early on, though. It seems, in years since, our enemy has been so blatant in his dark ways that people are starting to understand more of what they're up against. Still, not many know how to fight it, but necessity is the mother of invention."*

Again and again, the army of the dark one tried in vain to frighten the army of light, but to no avail. They were simply immovable. The more they tried to harm them, the more powerful they became. The love they possessed for those in the grip of darkness increased the more menacing the darkness was. As their rage was not having the effect they desired, they increased the intensity of their hatred. But to the soldiers of the light who were assured of victory, little else could penetrate their minds. It was only a matter of time.

For the army of the light, there was no back-up plan. The cost of losing was too great. Every soul mattered greatly to the Father and even those who had cursed them and tried to destroy their lives were fought for as hardily as though they'd been a good friend.

This strange army understood who their true enemy was and repeatedly forgave those who, although fighting against them, were indeed held captive by the army they served. It was difficult to miss the repulsive demons clinging to them, sucking the very life from them all the while telling them they were heroes and would be victorious. Unable to create, Satan had deceived them with copies of God's creation. Jealousy was his driving force. He had a PHD in it. The prince of defilement would infect anyone who gave him the opportunity. He hated God and wanted revenge so endeavored to destroy what Father held so dearly.

Beloved reasoned, *"Let me see if I've got it all correct now. You are to rescue those attacking you, who do not want to be rescued and don't even know they're in need of your help, while only striking at the demonic horde handling them, without using natural weapons... while being attacked by both."* She smiled a wide-eyed grin, *"Easy!"*

After it seemed that darkness had all but exhausted their cruelty, it was time for the light to take a turn and their weapon of choice was also their words. But, oh, what words they used!

Choosing their speech quite intentionally, these great warriors understood their power and used them with efficiency. They starting slowly, choosing every word with purpose and gaining momentum. As Holy Spirit captivated them, their light shone with great love.

Indeed, they were possessed by the power of Father's love, for He had equipped them with immeasurable weapons that held the power to change the world. The Father armed His soldiers with a tidal wave of His love. He had submerged them in it and then overwhelmed them again only to repeat it until they were completely enveloped. Love transformed all wounds and insecurities into armor to protect them - they were prepared for war!

Carrying the weight of love, their words originated in heaven and were felt immediately by the listener. The blessings of their heavenly Father were suddenly made tangible and had power to strip the dark of its grip and bring light to even the most wrathful person. Prepared by Papa God, this was the way of the intercessory-warrior!

Again and again, the words of the army of light were catapulted over to the enemy's captives. Words of light... love, peace, joy and truth landed with great brilliance on the heads of those held captive by the darkness and had a breathtaking effect on the receiver. Holy Spirit's powerful language accompanied every word with fire-bombs of glory. A blessing matched with every curse, the truth for every lie, love for bondage and peace for fear.

Launching the strength and power of heaven into the darkness, it paralyzed its targets at first. Then, slowly, it began to melt away the anger they felt, turning into glorious peace and remorse. Penetrating the shadows, their words expelled the lies of the enemy and healed wounds entangling them. Truly, they did not have a chance against the power of the light.

As you can imagine, with the light's superior weaponry increased by the authority of the Father, it would seem this war would more greatly resemble a decimation of the powers of darkness than a true war.

Rejoicing silently, Lord Jesus watched the victories the intercessors had with great joy. He'd intimately watched for years as the weight of doubt bombarded their faith. He had seen their faithful fight and endurance increasing with every battle. It had pleased Him more than words could say.

He remembered the treatment launched at those who followed His name, how they had been persecuted and hated for it. Now, it was clear just how much they'd been transformed. Their essential training had been completed, provided by the one whose jealous hatred wanted them dead.

"Yes, My friends-" Jesus laughed aloud. *"-quite a civil war."* He chided them. *"The Father has been working excitedly in anticipation for the awakening, washing His bride in His love for the world to see His great light. An awakened love-war!"* Lord Jesus related. *"But the awakening of His church will only be the beginning,"* Lord Jesus continued, *"because when they are prepared, He will bring home the prodigals. For, though they've been absent, they've never truly been apart from Him. In their darkest moments, in their most abandoned state, they couldn't help but love their heavenly Father as they felt His love for them. Even though they cursed Him, they couldn't help but love Him. Though they tried desperately to run from Him, He never left their side for a moment. He relentlessly pursued them in order to turn them back to Him.*

"My Father loves His prodigals. They are His secret weapon. Truly powerful, they know both the secrets of His heart and the secrets of the lost. They are the bridge that will link the two together. Our mission now is to unite the Lord's armies. For, I will redeem My bride at all costs."

The weight of intercession hit Beloved's heart with the impact of His words and she buried her face in her hands as she travailed in prayer. Doubling over, she knelt in the dirt surrounded by the wheat of the fields and felt the grace of it conferred to her. She was overwhelmed with intense love for Father's prodigal sons and daughters.

13

AWAKENING

DEEPLY CONTENTED IN the mesmerizing presence of her Lord and friend, Beloved prayed for the saints. Revelation from Father's Holy Presence fell on her heart like a thick blanket on a cold night. The familiar voice carried a message flooded with peace, yet held within it a firm resolve, echoing Lord Jesus... *"He will redeem His bride at all cost."*

Knowing Him as she did, she understood this meant war of some kind. It was only a matter of time until it would be revealed to her and, subsequently, all of human kind. She knew those who'd been prepared by fire would receive any battle with firm resolve, but those who had been told lies about the Great Father would be shaken to their core. The enemy had done his best to undermine the maturity of the church and inundated them with a heavy veil of pride and selfishness.

Again, Beloved was impressed with a burden to pray for the harvest. If there were to be a war, she did not want the lost to be hurt by it. As she prayed, God gave her a vision she couldn't quite understand. She saw the mountain of the Lord with a heavy fog emanating over the top. Over time, it increased, transforming into a thick cloud that contained the potential of something more to come, something that would affect the entire planet.

Beloved felt a heightened joy at the expectancy the vision brought to her as it rose in her heart, for surely it would be tangibly felt by those on Earth. She sensed it was Father's response to the prayers of the people and, through it, the world would know God as it never had before.

She was confident then in her perception of some impending danger, yet she had an overwhelming joy as she anticipated it. *This has to be it!* Her heart rejoiced. It would change everything she'd ever known about the Lord or the

154

earth. Truly, she did not understand what it was, but knew it would inevitably be the rescue they'd prayed for.

Lord Jesus put His hand on her shoulder. *"It is time."*

Instantly, she understood she was to go with Him. They must continue their journey.

Concealed by the wheat, they made it back to their horses as swiftly as possible. Resting easy under the shade of a large tree, the animals had waited faithfully and were ready to go. Setting out once again in the direction of Father's mountain, their journey was swift and made in record time.

Beautiful Time, the guardian of the entrance to the meeting place of the host, greeted them both with great dignity, as always. Yet, she hastily mentioned they'd been expected some time ago. Slipping through the familiar cave entrance, Beloved briefly took in the aroma of this wonderful place, enjoying the familiar memories of the cavern full of captivating stalactites hanging from the ceiling. She smiled as she remembered how she'd liked to refer to it as "the ballroom of crystal chandeliers."

Finally, they approached the door of the inner chamber where the prophetic host were assembled.

She was filled with exhilaration about seeing them again. It had been quite some time since all of them had been together. Since the debacle of the army of the great, they and Beloved had endured terrible trials that had altered each of them. It was a long and treacherous process for them. At times, it felt like death. Yet, the result of their troubles was soon to be evident, as she would see that each had been transformed into beautiful fire-warriors for the Lord.

As she hesitated before opening the door before them, the Lord placed a hand on her shoulder, reassuring her of His nearness. It was He Who'd requested this meeting and all were expected to be there. Indeed, who would miss it?

Entering the room, Beloved was hit with all the familiar, wonderful feelings again. She felt the impact of the inner room's tangible warmth, which was filled with a glowing amber light. Overwhelmed by the love and comfort of her very dear friends, her reservations gave way to joy. Helen, of course, was front and center and busy ushering forward the others of the prophetic host who'd been excited to greet the traveling pair.

It was like a thousand lovely family reunions, seeing all the wonderful faces and hearing all they had to share of their travels and trials. Finding comfort in their shared experiences and lessons learned, they visited for quite some time and would have liked to continue. When they were together, it gave them a little glimpse of heaven. Even so, they all knew they would have an eternity to spend with each other once their missions on Earth were completed.

Finally, Lord Jesus addressed the assembly of His faithful friends. *"Dear ones*," He said, pausing to secure the correct words, *"the time has come to accomplish the task you've all been prepared for."* He heaved a sigh of relief and smiled a smile that filled the room and every heart. The rest of what He said was a struggle to attend to as every mind was filled with the excitement of what they knew was ahead for them. Having prepared them so well in advance, there was little left unsaid but to encourage them in their mission.

Lost in her own thoughts, Beloved was shaken by the sudden somberness of the Lord's voice. *"My enemies tried to steal My bride from Me, friends. Indeed, I let them believe they could. I even worked to convince them of their power in order to reveal Myself through them. I used them to transform My bride and, surely, I have. She will rejoice in Me again as she once did, Seeking Me again and drawing herself close to Me. She will trust that I AM THE LORD!*

"I have kept you, My prophets, in reserve for this moment in time as a gift to My church. Your training in the secret place was under the strength of My hand. I have prepared you all for this hour, as you well know. I have refined you under the most intense pressure, for you will awaken and prepare My bride. Truly, you will teach My last-days-army the things I've taught you in secret, causing them to become the most radiant and powerful army that's ever been. All creatures of Heaven and Earth have awaited this hour: the hour in which the mystery of Father's extraordinary mercy will be truthfully understood.

"During this time, Father's Word will reveal His heart to the world and then they will know He is their Creator and God. Heaven's glory will dispel the shadows of doubt that cling to them and prepare them to know Me. They will love Me because of you and they will know Me because you know Me. I have been working hard to prepare you, My friends, to become a display of My kindness to the world. You've been washed of the selfish desire to be liked. Beautifully, you have shone brighter through your

trials. My light in its brilliance is undeniable - the world will see Me through you!

"Work now, for this is your time to fulfill what I've been anxious for you to accomplish. Do not look to seemingly important men for help; your answer is not there. Look only to Me and let Me envelope you in Myself. For, surely, you hold the answer to what the world is seeking. I will bring some mountains low, while raising other mountains high: expect this. I will continue to expose all the secrets and tools of My enemies. Expect this to happen and do not be afraid. Just remember it's your Father doing these things for you.

"Draw closer to Me. I long for your fellowship. You are My delight and I take great joy in you, My dear ones. Come to Me and I will renew your strength. All the promises I have made to you in past seasons you will believe in again. My prophesies will come to pass. My desires for you will be fulfilled. Renew yourself in Me. I'm calling to you now - Come!"

Jesus was graceful and elegant in His exhortation to the host, and all were wanting to share this moment with Him and rejoice in His hour. Truly, their joy could not be contained while they spent this time together, loving Him.

Sadly, Beloved's journey with Lord Jesus was coming to a close, for He was needed elsewhere. Still, she met her new journey with the host in joyful anticipation as they set out at once for a return trip to the enchanted meadow of deception, where the Lord's army slept.

Much of their travels were spent in rejoicing and sharing, but there was also much planning required and arrangements to be finished. None were really certain of what was to come, but Beloved had felt keenly that the vision she experienced of the coming glory was pertinent for this hour. Her cautious heart had kept her from sharing it, but it was ever present in the forefront of her thoughts.

As they traveled together for many days, passing through all the familiar places of Beloved's journey from several years previous, she was often distracted with old memories. Some were pleasant, while others held capsules of self reproach. But all recollection was conquered by the realization of her endurance. She'd come through so much. Lord Jesus had often reminded her that was the objective - not perfection, but breaking through. Along the way, others had labeled, slandered and misunderstood her. Some just didn't like her. However, the closer she drew to Lord Jesus, the less their opinions mattered. Through His eyes, she saw true reality and understood they were still blinded by the ways of the world and the deep sleep.

Helen sidled up alongside her, seeing her heavy eyes. *"It's amazing how easily the inactive mind takes us back to joyless places, isn't it?"*

Shaken from her self-imposed history course, Beloved was instantly smiling again when she felt Helen's thin arm wrap itself through hers. *"Oh, Helen,"* she interjected, *"how much we've all gone through."* She stopped herself from saying more. Her mind was full of questions of the future, as she remembered the vision of glory and dug for an understanding of what Jesus meant when He said He would win His bride at ALL COSTS.

Smiling and enjoying the very best company, she rejoiced to hear her friends' advice. *"So often,"* Helen began slowly, *"I have found that the things Father has shown me in part would become a lot less worrisome when put together with the reality of their materialization."*

Beloved understood her meaning and felt comfort in her understanding. Looking up through her bright eyes, she smiled at her with a heart revived. Somehow, Helen understood the battle of her worries, and Beloved wondered if she'd seen a similar vision.

After some time, Helen halted. *"Look!"* she whispered in excitement. *"We are finally here again!"*

Beloved was instantly lost in a flood of memories. Before she'd left this dreadful place of enchantment to find the prophetic host, the angels who watched over those here had asked for her help. Here she was again, and with the host she'd sought to aid her. She remembered those sleeping whom she'd tried to minister to while here: a woman who struggled with guilt from an abortion in her teen years, and a man who'd labored under the weight of his own success. She felt the burden of their plight still, yet now with hope lifting her heart as she was certain that somehow their needs would be answered.

A field of poisoned flowers - indeed, the oppression of the world's system - had lulled them to sleep. They were asleep to the reality of God and could only see Him through glimpses as their lives were oppressed by their world's agendum. Meant to become kings and priests unto their God, instead they were led down a path of futility, becoming cogs in a wheel of the sinister system that clouded even the minds of the church, lulling them into a deep sleep.

On entering the meadow of the enchantment, the host inspected the sleeping army and found it just as it had been. All were deeply unaware of the reality they were missing.

The conversation soon turned to making plans and offering suggestions. Devising their first order of business, they sought Father for guidance and knelt down in among the sleeping people. Their prayers transformed the atmosphere and involuntarily turned to exalted praise.

Suddenly, they were made aware of millions of angels all around them. Guarding them as well as the sleeping army, the elysian watchmen could not hold back and joined the host as their voices rang out. It seemed as if something were bolstering their praise and it was unlike anything the worshipers had ever experienced. A Mighty Wind was empowering their words of exultation and tremendous momentum was wrapping itself in and through them as they were caught up in rapturous praises to Father God!

I give You praise with an open heart.
I'm waking up to heaven, I'm waking up to You!

I choose this day to be grateful Lord.
I give You praise with an open heart.
I'm waking up to heaven, I'm waking up to You!
Your faithfulness like the sunrise.
Your endless love reaches past the skies.
I'm waking up to heaven, oh, I'm waking up to
*You!*₁)*

They roared out praise into the heavens with arms lifted high. Their worship filled the meadow with the boldness and authority gained through the fire. They wept as the moment of their journey had arrived. Throwing off their restraints, they danced as David had long ago.

What a tremendous moment! Beloved thought. Enraptured in majestic exaltation, a flickering question flashed through her mind. *I wonder why the angels are singing?* No sooner had the question entered her mind than she remembered the vision of glory that Holy Spirit had given her. *Were they here for that?* she wondered.

Suddenly, thunder blast through the atmosphere as if to join in with their rhapsodic extolment. As it acted as a crescendo to their worship, a bright-white lightning filled the night sky. They marveled as the sky above transformed into a massive, majestic storm. As though the earth were responding to something in the heavens, trees swirled in a grand dance as the ground under them shook. The sky became dark and foreboding as it was filled with the Almighty's power.

A monumental cloud formed above their heads as the intense thunder that shook the earth reacted to the collected lightning. Inside of the storm cloud were thousands of angelic creatures who swirled in and out of the glory as it increased, calling to something and communicating with it. As if responsive to the calling for His glory, the fire bolts of His Spirit answered in reply, rising up into an immeasurable wave as high as the mountain itself.

As the wave rose, Beloved could not help but feel an incredible expectancy rise in her heart. She knew this was a wave of the Spirit rising high above the earth. Upon its ascension, it held itself there for a lengthy moment, as Father Himself filled their hearts with wonder at His might and power. Surely, there was none greater than the Lord, no, not one. She trusted in Him as a small child trusted the love of a dear parent, and she knew that life and death would be joyous if left in His lone hands.

"It is here!" she cried as she raised her hands toward the heavens in awestruck wonder.

An overwhelming wave of what she knew to be shimmering, golden, pearlescent glory rose up from the mountain of the Lord in the distance. Gushing up and expanding in sheer magnitude, it reached high above and beyond Earth's atmosphere. With an involuntary shriek of glee, Beloved threw her hands out in anticipation as the wave came plunging toward them. In the next instant, it broke over the expanse of the planet.

Beloved stood, arms outstretched, and cried tears of exuberance as she laughed with a heart full of Father's promise kept. For the first time in her life, she felt the very essence of Truth flood her. Her eyes were completely open to the wonder of God. All at once, she understood that she was desperately loved without *any* reservation. Though she was created for an earthly mission, she was truly the daughter of the *Most High*. Any trace of the accuser's lies was washed from her by the total wholeness she felt.

Helen's arms were suddenly around her shoulders, as her dear friend had remembered her. *"Beloved,"* she cried! *"Beloved!"* Overwhelmed by tears of joy, they held each other while dancing in joy as Shekinah glory rained down on them.

Closing her eyes, Beloved savored the weight of this momentous event she'd long awaited, and forefelt the moment's ending. But, to her surprise, she opened her eyes to find it all around her. Covering the earth in glistening golden glory deposited by the enormous wave of Holy Spirit, it was a new and fresh dispensation for the earth.

"Glory!" Beloved screamed. *"It was His glory I saw in the vision!"*

Gleefully rejoicing together, understanding flooded them all. *"This was the coming dispensation of the Lord! It is here at last!"*

Questions flooded their discourse. What would the effects of this occurrence be? Would it change things for the battle over the river of shame? Of course, it would. It would change everything! Of course! Of course!

The Shekinah glory overwhelmed the earth with a Divine fragrance that changed the atmosphere everywhere. They felt Father's strength, and with it they were suddenly alive with His purpose for the planet, ever so much more than before.

Many suddenly remembered those sleeping in the enchanted flowers at their feet, and turned their attention upon them. One woman let out a scream.

As others were drawn to her, she stood shocked, with her hands held against her mouth. *"Father God!"* she squealed. *"Father God! Oh, Father, oh, precious Father!"* Others rushed to her aid.

"Oh, God! Oh, dear God!" a man yelled as he turned himself around and doubled over in a barrage of tears. *"Yes!"* others shrieked. *"Yes! It's happened, oh, God, thank you, thank you, thank you!"* Then, as others began to understand what was happening, multitudes of those sleeping were rising up out of the flowers. And as sleep tried to cling to them, they were forced to sit up, wondering what was happening to them.

"Oh, Jesus!" Beloved cried as others rushed to the aid of those awakening! God's glory had awakened them. Their eyes were opening. The world had changed! God's power was poured on a thirsty land and the sleep of the enemy was losing its grip on the minds of mankind.

The Father's army was at last awakening, and the prophetic host was busy gathering the spoils of their great victory, together again, with many more to come. God had kept His promise!

(1)*
https://www.azlyrics.com/lyrics/upperroom/youandyoualone.html

14

THE PRODIGALS RETURN

AFTER QUITE SOME time of rejoicing and ministry, they decided it was best, at last, to remove themselves from the place of enchantment. Together, the host and the now awakened army headed back through the fields of grace in hopes of joining Lord Jesus there. While they traveled, Beloved busied her mind with examining all that had changed since the glory had arrived. Pride, fear, and self-seeking rebellion were suddenly exchanged for wisdom, divine knowledge, obedience without fear and the blessings of peace and joy. But Beloved couldn't help wondering what else may have changed.

She remembered Lord Jesus saying, *"As the prodigals return, they will bring such rejoicing to the church that it will be tempting for them to think they've won the war completely, yet it will be only the beginning."* He said He would light the torch of their lives to illuminate the nations. The enemy would come to fight and find himself losing the souls of those he prized most.

While traveling back to the fields of grace, they were met by a small crowd of people spilling out onto the road before a small one-room bar. Unable to pass by without inquiring about the ruckus taking place, one of the gentlemen of the host approached the back of a young man near the rear of the crowd, *"Hey friend, what is it that is going on here? Is everything alright?"*

"For sure, man! It's all God! Wow!" He wiped his brow to keep from being overrun by his emotions. *"I just never knew God was like this! I just never knew."* He couldn't talk anymore as he was overcome with feeling. Whether doubled over

in grief or something like relief, they could not quite make out.

Speaking for the great company, the gentleman went on to question a young woman, who seemed a bit more in control of her emotions. With great enthusiasm, she replied, *"Sir, have you not seen the miracles done in this place? Oh, I see you are not from here, are you? God is moving, sir. He is moving! Brian, over there-"* she pointed to the front of the crowd. *"-has been an alcoholic for years, suffering from depression and family trouble. Well, he went crazy when that gold stuff landed in the bar. He jumped on the table all excited like and started screaming for us all to repent. He was going crazy! Just crazy! He said that he'd been raised in church and knew what the gold meant and he was afraid for us and wanted us to stop sinning and stuff. We weren't sure what to think, but then old George walked in and... old George had been a quadriplegic for 30 years from an accident when he was young. Anyway! You don't get it do you, sir? Old George walked in! We were all like, 'ahhhh!' But Brian started screaming at us and told us it was God and that we'd better get right with Him. Many of us were raised in church but not a church like Brian's. His must have been just unreal or something!"* Feeling she had explained enough, she turned back around because she didn't want to miss out on anything.

The company had seen enough as well, this was fantastic! Several of them ran to the front to help the young man who was preaching, for there were many who'd been overcome by the Spirit already and many more who'd been healed of diseases.

It was just like many of the old-time tent revivals Beloved had heard of - alive with such transformation that it took her a while to realize that this bar was not far from where her brother lived. Yearning, she searched for him in the crowd. At last, she asked several of the people in the gathering only to discover many knew him, but he hadn't been at the bar for quite some time. Beloved was so hoping to see him again. For years, she'd been praying for her brother and hoped at last he'd have a chance to find the peace he'd needed so desperately in his life. With a sigh, she entrusted him to the Lord once more.

Before long, it was decided that some of the host should stay behind to help the prodigals as the outpouring was becoming more than the locals could deal with. Remarkably, quite a few of the prodigals decided to travel on with them to the fields of grace to share their experiences. Everyone rejoiced and set out with fresh excitement for the future!

The exhilaration of those experiencing miracles at the bar had given her new evidence of what God was doing on the earth. Beloved was overcome with delight and couldn't stop praising Him. Yet, now as they returned to their travels, the old worries about the impending battle returned. But as it wasn't something she could do anything about, she offered it up to Father and continued with the joyous company.

"I've just had too much time to think on our travels," she reasoned, trying to shake it off.

Finally reaching the outer edges of the vast fields of grace, she and the others were taken aback by what seemed to be a treacherous storm in the distance. Giddy with new joy, the prodigals and many of the last-day warriors had gone ahead of the prophetic host, for they were anxious to see what they'd only heard about.

Now, as the remainder of the company approached the fields of grace, they were met by two of their members who'd rushed on ahead of them with the excited prodigals. It seemed the prodigals had met with trouble as they'd traveled through the fields. Some of those working there had risen up against them and tried to throw them out. The newly awakened last-day army were appalled and couldn't believe that those whose return had been celebrated by Father would be dealt with such harsh treatment by those in the fields of grace.

Beloved felt something rising in her spirit all the while, *"Was this what caused the anxiety in my spirit?"* she wondered.

Considering her next move, she remembered the Word of God and the story Lord Jesus often told of the prodigal son finally returned and the older brother, who was offended by his father's response. He refused to receive the return of his brother with joy because he did not understand that neither he nor his family would be whole until his wayward brother was fully restored to his previous place among them.

Indeed, she reasoned, what the older brother and so many others didn't understand was that sin carries a heavy burden, and the sinner naturally bears the weight of the curse it brings into their life. It is a terrible heaviness that torments a soul and leaves a person to cope in unusual ways. Some fight against it by hating God or people, but their true war is with themselves and they must battle to receive the hope they're offered.

Just at that moment, Maria Woodworth-Etter came walking from the fields to meet with Beloved once again. *"Welcome, my dear friend. I have been expecting you all today. How was your journey?"*

Laboring to get the better of her anxiety for the troubled prodigals, she replied, *"It was just fine, sister. It's good to be back and very nice to be met by you. In fact, I am very glad you came..."*

"Beloved," the woman of God interrupted, *"do you remember when I told you there were corpses in the fields?"*

"Yes," Beloved smiled at the mention of it.

"There are many dead people in the church. They are bitter and full of thorns. Do you believe they can be raised to life?"

Honestly, Beloved wanted to reply no, but she knew the answer had already been made in the Scriptures. Ezekiel had been asked the same question, so she repeated his answer, *"Only the Lord knowest."*

Maria nodded with a friendly smile and turned back to the fields to leave.

"Wait, sister!" Beloved called after her. Ms. Etter paused and turned to her.

"How can believers fight during a time of such unprecedented glory being manifest? Shouldn't the glory change every heart?"

"Good question, Beloved. But remember, the same sun that melts butter will harden clay."

"Thank you, Ma'am. I understand," Beloved responded. *"We are all responsible for the decisions of our own hearts."*

Maria answered back, *"Truly, and there is joy in taking responsibility for our actions because we can decide that, with God's help, we'll not do it again - it gives us hope! Too many of your generation have tried to remove the shame of sin before it has a chance to do its work in the human heart. In my generation, we prayed for sinners to feel conviction like the woman with the alabaster jar in the Bible. We knew it would be something they'd never want to feel again. It drew them to the Lord because only He can truly wipe away their sin. If we rob them of taking responsibility, they will harden like clay and become prideful and judgmental of others who struggle, for he who is forgiven much, loves much. Indeed, he who is forgiven only a little does not have much love at all."*

"You were talking earlier of the older brother, Beloved. Yes, the older brother stayed of his own accord. He felt the father should have loved him more than the prodigal because he was good. But it was never a competition and their father loved them both the same. This has always been the trouble and it hardens the hearts of believers to reason it. Some who feel the weight of their judgment against the prodigals will melt in submission to Father's joy, but those who feel justified by their own works will not be willing to submit and there's only one thing that can be done."

"Beloved," Maria said as she reached for her hand, looking her in the eyes with secret meaning, *"you must protect the prodigals. Death to self means true life."* She smiled a broad smile and turned again to reenter the fields.

On traveling into the fields of grace, the vast company of the host, prodigals and awakened army were instantly overwhelmed by hundreds of angry believers who wanted something to be done about the prodigals. In their estimation, they were just a big problem. *"They are too crazy,"* they bellowed, *"and must be subdued. They're bothering the corpses! They're just foolish, loud and too much trouble!"*

Beloved listened with wide eyes, almost wanting to laugh. *"Okay, I'll check into it,"* she answered. She knew better than to let them know she didn't take them seriously. With this reply, they walked off feeling as though they'd done a wise and noble thing, for such is the nature of self-righteousness.

The host immediately gathered for prayer and, asking Holy Spirit for guidance and strength, they felt a resurgence of the power and assurance they needed.

Upon approaching the prodigals, they found many of them were crying and visibly shaken by the anger and hostility they had met with in the fields of grace. They had been told of the peace and tranquility it would bring them, but what a disappointment hit them when they were not loved as Jesus loved them.

Yet, with the arrival of the prophetic host, a great heave of relief was felt in the awakened army for the sake of the prodigals with them. They knew the prophets were courageous and would know just how to handle the naysayers, for the fire had made them fearless and pain had given them wisdom.

Immediately, the confrontation was turned from the prodigals to the host. The self-righteous were all over them in an instant. In their estimation, God's kingdom was at stake and it was all the fault of these crazy prophets. They felt justified in their rage and ignoble in their treatment of everyone. After all, in their minds, they were defending nothing less than all of Christendom!

"Listen," Beloved shouted to them, *"this cannot be!"* She demanded their silence. *"What we have done is in direct order of Holy Spirit. And these whom Lord Jesus has saved will never be turned away as long as there is breath in my body. We-"* She turned to show her strength of force in the last-day army and the host *"-will never allow you to bully these who've been tread down by your hostility before and only now returned to find Lord Jesus again."* Beloved continued, *"NO! This will be their day. Not only will I not throw them out, I will throw them a party!"*

Shrieks and screams of unearthly nature sounded from the Christian-corpses. Surely, they had not been motivated by Lord Jesus but for themselves and had been open prey for any of the demonic who'd wanted to claim them. And claim them they had. They were filled with such rage and fear that it startled even Beloved. She knew then

Maria was right. The prodigals needed to be protected from them and their demons.

Turning in a rage, they spewed their curses at the prodigals and felt vengeful, already making plans of how to avenge themselves. *"You've not heard the last of us, you … you heretics! False prophets!"* And with that, they left the fields of grace. Their response was more violent than Beloved had anticipated and she hoped they would not fall prey to the false bride. She began to wonder if she had been too hard on them, but she had seen what damage could be done by such thinking.

However, as most of the crowd dispersed, she was suddenly surrounded by some of the corpses on their knees. Crying profusely, they grabbed her hands and started pleading for forgiveness. *"We are so sorry for our behavior. Thank God you came and showed us the brutality of our thinking. We want no more of it - we want Jesus. We need Him! We need His freedom and we want to love again."*

Beloved knelt down with them in the wheat and dust of the fields, crying with them as all of the host knelt as well. With much embracing, they welcomed them gratefully into their ranks and were glad that some dry bones had found new life.

From the back of the crowd, a man made his way to where they were kneeling and watched them eagerly. All he did was watch them. Upon noticing him, Beloved felt she knew him, searching her mind for recognition. He was a young man, not old, but somehow she felt she had known him as an older man.

He seemed quite happy with all that had taken place, as he'd been watching them for some time. When, at last he turned to smile at her, she knew for certain and was thrilled!

"You are Brother Bob Jones, aren't you?!" she squealed.

The crowd turned at that, all eyes on him.

Beloved jumped to her feet and rushed to his side. *"You too!"* she exclaimed. *"First Sister Maria, and now you! Oh, my goodness!"*

With effervescent joy that filled the crowd, he laughed over her excitement, and thought her reply was very funny. *"What a mighty victory you've had, Beloved. You all have, haven't you? What a mighty victory! It's clear to me you have all learned how to love! I'm so thankful Papa God let me see it- so thankful. I've been praying for it for so many years and now, at last, I can see it happening. That's the difference between the goats and the sheep."* He laughed again. *"They ain't got no love in 'em. You can always tell a goat-Christian by how they treat the prodigals - that's one thing to look for. Their fruit shows up eventually. And they sure do hate the prophets too, don't I know that!"* He continued to belly laugh and led them to rejoice in it all.

Beloved could not get over his presence there, for he'd been in heaven many years. Indeed, much of the prophetic host had known him, as his prophesies were still much referenced. All were very pleased to be afforded this meeting.

"Father let me come to you," he continued, *"to give you all a message. Are you ready for it?"*

"Yes," they agreed whole-heartedly.

"Father wanted me to ask you all: Is fear your God? Papa said to remind you that I have not given you a spirit of fear but of love, power and a sound mind. Many of you have been really attacked by the devil. You have seen his power, but Papa doesn't want you to forget that He has power over him. Whatever you face in the future, remember this." He hesitated a moment. *"Greater is He Who is in you than the evil that's in the world today. If you disobey Lord Jesus for fear of your enemy, fear has become your god, hasn't it? Father wants you to obey only Him and only fear your disobedience to Him, for it's*

the only thing that can stop you. Nothing can hurt you at all really, because you got the Lord. Even death can't trouble you when you got the Lord."

He seemed relieved as he finished. *"That's it, kids,"* he said with a broad smile.

The host assured him of their understanding and felt grateful for his warning. *"God is so good!"* many said. Helen most assuredly felt it and it put her heart to rest of an uneasiness that had been troubling her. She and Beloved gave each other an understanding smile.

Brother Bob wanted to greet all those who'd repented at Father's bidding and were full of the fresh tears and raw love mercy brings. Then he, too, left them again, for he'd fulfilled his mission.

Many other miracles were experienced after the new dispensation had taken place. Many they never expected had turned to God and *"melted"* as Sister Maria would say. Many millionaires came to know Lord Jesus and gave away their mansions, becoming friends with ex-criminals, who rushed to give away the money they'd made from their crimes in order to save more souls.

It was all overwhelming to Beloved and continually brought her to tears by the goodness of God. The feeling of dread that had prodded her spirit was turned to expectation since Brother Bob's visit.

"*God wouldn't have given me an army,*" she reasoned, "*unless He knew I'd need one.*" She knew now that whatever they'd face, Father would be with them. Lord Jesus would have the victory and they would share in His joy!

15

INVADING FORCES

WHILE DRIVING BACK the hostile enemies of salvation, the fields of grace became a place of wild activity and many thousands were added to their ranks daily. Everyone, even the newest Christian, was winning souls at an unprecedented rate. It seemed to Beloved that the church had become what it was always meant and she praised God for it.

The host was busy training the Lord's last-days army and had already taken several reconnaissance missions to the river of shame. Plans were being made, but not without much prayer and seeking Holy Spirit's counsel. Beloved felt they had almost reached the pinnacle of joy together in this marvelous place. Trust in Lord Jesus was at an all-time high and the miracles and salvation were evidence of it.

Yet, while they rejoiced, their joy could never be complete until the lost had been restored to Father and the ranks of the accuser had been decimated. As the warriors of Christ began to realize the negative effect the war was having on the lost in the river, they set up special camps of intercession for those still held captive by the repugnant dark waters. Without those, the enemy turned every victory won into something dark and menacing, sending even more fear into the river of shame. Attempting to head-off the attack the enemy knew must be soon, he unloaded his rage on those he held in his grip. Still kept in a tranquilized state, their lives were in jeopardy until they could be redeemed by the Lamb and restored to Father.

Along with so many others, Beloved hungered for the deliverance of the captives. Some would try at times to venture out to redeem them to the Father, assuring them repeatedly of His love for them. Sadly, they were often thwarted by witches causing offense and fear, twisting care and concern into something dark and insidious. Offense was used again and again to suppress their freedom, keeping their rage as hot as possible. The evil ones kept them focused on lies, filling their minds until they were made efficient tools to repel the light and love of Father's kingdom. Their slander worked to disparage the children of God and cause their counsel to be rebuffed.

As the church grew daily, and more and more prodigals returned, it was tempting to think they were experiencing the last-days revival so many had prophesied. Yet, there was still much preparation to be done. Even so, the prophetic host had experienced great strides in training both the army of the prodigals and the last-days army. Even more recently, the army of children had returned to the fields and were taking up supportive roles in the training being done.

What joy those blessed children brought to all the camps as they delivered many from traumas incurred in their past. Spending time with them was such a joy for Beloved too. She'd always felt like a delighted older sister to them and took pride in all their accomplishments. The angelic loved to play with them as well, for, to them, they were as familiar as breathing.

However, no joy or victory they experienced could be as sweet as it should be to her due to the agony of those held captive in that dreadful river. She'd been with them and felt their pain. The experience had never left her and had been the driving force of all she'd been through and accomplished for her Lord. Lord Jesus had bid all of them wait for Him there in the fields and she was assured of His soon arrival, but it had been quite some time since she'd seen Him.

One day, Beloved saw a crowd surrounding a small white church nestled in the wheat. It was not often used since the crowds had surpassed its capacity long ago. Still, many warriors sought it out as a special place to seek the Lord. As she rounded the corner of the front, she was surprised to find the Great Eagle again, even larger than before. He was busy depositing large quantities of kindling wood around the base of the outside of the church and had nearly finished when Beloved arrived.

Addressing him, she asked, *"What are you doing with the firewood around this church?"*

"Preparing to light a fire, Beloved."

She understood him, and laughed. He wasn't going to give away His secrets. *"Alright. Well, I am very pleased to see you again,"* Beloved ended.

"And I you," He answered warmly, stopping for a moment to let her know He cared for her. *"The Father has plans for this church. That is all I can tell you for now. Soon, all will be known."*

"Also, Beloved," He continued, *"I wanted to tell you that the prodigals with you are more useful than you may realize. They carry keys and information that will be beneficial to you as you invade the river of shame. I would investigate what they know, if I were you. You may be pleased with what you hear."*

"Of course! I would be happy to hear of it! Thank you so much. I'll let you get back to your work. Blessings to you!" Beloved was excited by what He'd told her and left to look into immediately.

On venturing back to camp, she noticed just how keen the prodigals were in refining their skills as warriors and learning the Word. She was already very impressed with them and grateful to have so many of them come to help.

Beloved remembered the truth she'd told herself so many times. *If one were not a threat, the enemy would not be attacking.*

The prodigals are targeted by the enemy because they are a threat to him. What makes them so dangerous to him? She wondered.

Approaching a few of the prodigals who'd joined together in front of their camp area, she found them taking refreshment together. She enjoyed watching their laughter, for it was as free as a lost young lamb who has just been rescued from a storm.

"Beloved!" they shouted as they rose to greet her. *"What are you doing here, Ma'am?"*

"Funny you should ask. While talking to the Great Eagle," motioning to the church, she continued, *"He mentioned there may be some key or bit of information you have that would help in our mission to invade the dark waters. I decided to set off immediately to speak with you."*

The group of young ones immediately burst into laughter. It seemed they'd just been praying for God to make a way for them to share what they'd been thinking about. *"You see, Beloved,"* one of them began, *"this is our battle - our revenge! Satan has taken a lot from us and it has made us hate him with a vengeance. But he has also put a lot in us. Meaning, we know how he ticks. We know how the lost are thinking and what may frighten them or help them understand. We felt we should share some of the things we know about the power of darkness as well."*

"Absolutely!" Beloved answered. *"Let us go together and find the host. You can share what you know with them."*

Together with Beloved, the prodigals outlined their strengths and how they felt they could be of help. They would be, indeed, a force for the enemy to reckon with. After all, it was through him this great army was formed, as each warrior was fashioned by the devil's own handiwork. Every bondage and bruise he had inflicted on them, every episode of painful rejection and humiliation, Jesus was able to transform into a powerful weapon aimed at Satan's kingdom.

Certainly, understanding their power over him must make him anguish at the thought of what he'd lost. He considered them stripped of all their treasure and reduced to trash. After trying to rob them of their calling and identity, instead of succeeding in his attempted annihilation, Jesus would use it all to make them the very ones who would be his undoing. And through his evil efforts to kill and destroy, he had created his own worst nightmare - redeemed souls bent on his destruction.

Indeed, one by one, he must look on their familiar faces, seeing all he'd labored to destroy had now become weapons turned against him. He must well know these enemy-seeking-warriors were not naive as they once were, but understood his schemes quite well. Having inside insight as to how he operated, these great warriors would not be beguiled by selfish ambition and pride. Having walked through the fires of affliction, they shone with the radiance of the restored. Fearless because they'd suffered all that hell had thrown at them, they lived for the One Who loved them, for the kingdom and the Lamb.

In one glance, Satan would see those he had tried to destroy...would wound him.

Continuing for some time, they shared all the secrets of the dark arts that they themselves had used to destroy many Christian families and draw their children into darkness. They shared details of how Christians could become armed against the strategies of witches and the incantations launched against them. The soldiers of the Lord would finally become wise to the schemes and strategies of darkness that had made their work so difficult and held the lost in the grip of shame.

After hours and hours of conversation, it was clear the prodigals were perfect to be the very ones who could reach the lost. All they'd been through had left its mark on them and through that it would bring ease to those who were still caught in the dark river. Hope was their lifeline and it would be received because of the shared experiences of their pasts. Those so recently saved from the world of lies would understand the bondage that held them.

Beloved was so excited by this tremendous breakthrough. This was what she'd prayed and hoped for. *"We do not battle with flesh and blood, but for it!"* she cheered. *"Our battle is with unseen forces and He Who is Faithful and True will deliver them to us. AMEN!"* She shouted as she left the meeting, leaving behind the host who were thoroughly wrapped up in all the prodigals had to show them.

She was so excited, but one thing was still missing. *"Oh, Lord!!! Where are you?"* she spoke up into the heavens, impatient for Him to arrive and lead them.

At that moment, she felt a tap on her shoulder and whirled around excitedly.

"Lord!" she exclaimed. *"Lord!"* Throwing herself into His arms, she hugged Him tightly *"I'm so glad You're here. I was just thinking about You."*

"I know!" He said with a laugh, *"I'm right here, Beloved. That's where I am!"*

Beloved started to chatter away to Him as she always had in past, wanting to fill Him in on all their activities, of which He was already familiar, of course. Suddenly, she stopped short and backed away from Him. First, she was distracted by the magnificent steed standing next to Him, then by the massive crowd of angels hovering all around Him. Millions of angelic beings filled the skies over the fields of grace as far into the distance as she could see. *"Oh!"* Beloved gasped. *"You've got company!"*

Taking it all in, she was overcome with the sight of them all. It was as if heaven had come to Earth and all she could do was marvel at it. She saw many familiar faces in the crowd as she'd been aided by them in past and, recognizing her, they acknowledged the friendship.

All of those in the fields of grace were struck with the magnificence of heaven's army, only able to gape in amazement. And what a wonder the field was to behold, with the prophetic host, the last-days army, the prodigals, the army of children and the great army of heaven's warriors. All Father's soldiers were, together at last, rejoicing in the splendor of one another. What joy was created in seeing it!

Beloved stood back to survey the spectacle of all the camps and warriors brought together here in this glorious place she loved so much. These were *God's* five armies, all encamped at the river's edge ready for battle and all for the sake of those she'd longed to see transformed and saved by Lord's life abundance.

"We are in reach," she thought to herself. *"We are indeed! Now, it begins!"*

16

RETURN TO THE
RIVER OF SHAME

BRILLIANTLY, LORD JESUS set to work full of expectant delight. He met with key leaders of every army and gave them Father's instructions and guidance. All were prayed with, empowered by Holy Spirit and sent away, each having left with an altogether different countenance than when they'd entered His presence. They were filled with a bold confidence, like young lions ready and waiting to be unleashed to fight. Old men, young men, old women and young, working together as one, all understanding the cost as well as the reward of their war against darkness. Each counted securely on the other as well as Lord Jesus, their Champion and King. Truly, He was the bold Ruler of all kings and no apostate usurper could take His place!

Taking up their positions with confidence, all armies were stationed and ready as their moment had at last arrived. Assembled in resplendent unity, all were waiting for Lord Jesus and His command.

Assuring Him of their readiness, they cried out. One, then another, then more until all cried out in exceeding joy that penetrated the atmosphere. It was so thunderous, it caused the ground to shake: "FOR THE KINGDOM OF GOD AND FOR THE LAMB, OUR CHRIST!"

Lord Jesus was deeply moved to tears of joy and pride. Shouting back to them, He cried in a bold, powerful voice, *"MAKE READY!"* He watched as the armies shifted positions, intensity filling their ranks.

"This is it!" Beloved mused as she waved her banner proudly.

"GOOOOOOOOOOOOOOOO!!!" the White Horse Rider shouted with a voice like a trumpet

blast and a thunder crash. All the earth responded to His triumphant shout!

Like a bullet unleashed from a gun was the power and speed in which these five armies shot out from the safety of the fields of grace and eagerly entered the realms of darkness. Horses, chariots, wagons, arrows and engines, bullets and guns could not have equaled such an army as this. With the speed of heaven's warriors above, they ran and rode hard to the river of shame.

They entered the dark forest possessed by witches who controlled the demonic and the atmosphere prevailing there, yet were unaffected. Having been given helpful keys from the prodigals, they climbed its hills and valleys with relative ease, boldly reaching the ravine that overlooked their destination. Stationed side by side, the great company stood peering out over its embankments and saw what some had only heard about.

Startlingly repugnant, thick black substance that looked more like tar than water held the captives. It was a river of countless imprisoned souls held in its clutches. Demons, unaware of the presence of the armies, bludgeoned and whipped their prisoners. Small, peevish creatures who, when seen, would not promote fear, were disgustingly delighted in their own depravity. Savoring the fear they caused, loving the self-hatred they promoted, they reminded each soul of the shamefulness of their sin and desperate fear that gripped their minds. The sky was dark, and the air was unbearable to breathe as clouds rolled ominously over the waters, teeming with Father's lost children, hardly recognizable.

At the entrance of the river was an enormous statue that possessed the head of a cow and the body of a man set on a large box with a simple door in the front. He was the king of shame, holding Father's creations under his control to pervert and manipulate. *This was the enemy's secret weapon.*

Beloved's eyes were opened to the idol's machinations. This was how the river had managed to gain such vast influence. She watched as everyone, young and old, entered the river through the small door in the center of the base of the statue. Before they entered, they were full of life, but they exited as shells of their former selves. Though it was apparent it appeared as nothing more than an innocent box to them, they were subjected to a whole world abandoned to denigration. Addicted to its pull, they were admitted over and over, exposed to continuous waves of perversion. Generations became zombies. For, led by the voices of the box, they were poisoned repeatedly with deception. Created to be kings and priests unto God, the statue made them hate themselves instead.

Stripped of the hope and innocence of youth, they were left with utter despair, with no confidence in their future. The box was indoctrinating them, telling them what to think, what emotions to feel, all under the guise of entertainment. In reality, it was nothing but poison, telling them God's reality was a lie and only Satan's reality was actual truth. Holding their minds in numb captivity, they were bombarded constantly with demonically projected images reinforcing death's agenda.

As the five armies studied the river below, their ranks were jolted from the vivid scene and were suddenly alive with activity. *"What? How? Who?"* Were the questions that spread through their ranks as their attention was drawn to a small group of people who fought at the river's edge to retrieve its captives. *"Who are those already fighting at the river's edge?"*

Beloved looked to see what they were all talking about. A small band of struggling warriors worked tirelessly at the river's edge, dragging soul after soul out of the grip of the river while enduring relentless attacks from the demonic. Fighting with courage and great passion, only a handful of people struggled to rescue them, one by one.

All eyes turned to Lord Jesus with inquisitive looks, but His eyes were on Beloved. And as her eyes met His, she was full of questions. Looking again at the dark water, she suddenly realized who these warriors were. In amazement, she saw it was the man she'd seen watching her as she traveled through the river with the Lord years ago. Having watched her eagerly, jealously, this man had longed for the relationship she had with the Lord. It was Daniel, Beloved's lost brother, whom she'd searched for repeatedly. He was here and had betrayed the river, now leading others to do so as well.

Her eyes instantly filled with tears as she bent over with emotion. *"Daniel?"* she questioned the Lord.

"Yes, Beloved," He answered. *"He has been here all along. Indeed, he has been working here with Me since the day we left and he is almost worn out. But he has been successful and has been waiting for you. Indeed, all of you,"* He said as He glanced toward the armies there.

Beloved was overcome with emotion as she watched her brother continue to labor, unaware of their arrival.

Yet, they, too, were caught unaware, for while they had hesitated at the ravine, a large black creature shot out at them with an army of thick blackness behind it. It was the Babylonian false-bride Beloved had encountered in the forest. Masquerading as a new-world-Christianity, the witch of a bride was there to fight for possession of her stolen goods!

She was larger now and more emboldened than before. It seemed the army that followed her in the train of her blackened gown possessed ranks filled to capacity. Hovering above the river of shame, she was at eye level with the five armies and her four vacant black eyes looked to Beloved, glaring again at her with two abhorrent faces as if she was ready to partake of a great feast. Examining the armies who'd joined together to fight against her, the false bride saw many other familiar faces in the ranks of the well-loved. All of them were repugnant to her now and she looked on them with disgust, like a bad memory leaving an equally bad taste in her mouths.

She was now wearing a large, oval shaped, three-tiered tiara, adorned in sapphires, rubies and emeralds topped with an ornate globe. She carried herself like a beautiful queen, but was hideous and odd. Her hair was matted and unkempt, full of creatures as hateful as death while her gown, black and shredded, trailed behind her in a train of demonized creatures who equaled her fury. Yet, it was her eyes, empty, black and monstrous, that starkly clashed with the richness of her tiara. But to her it was all gloriously splendid and made her powerful and strong.

The false bride opened her mouths to speak and her voice rang out like a hundred voices speaking all at once, reverberating through a thousand cold, hollowed caves. She expected her presence to settle over the armies like a tyrant's dagger with oppressive fear, but she would be disappointed. They were unlike any army she'd faced in the past - they were the bride of Christ.

Suddenly, a humble man of unmarked rank declared to the witch, *"Our Father, Elohim, has promised us an inheritance; it is our destiny! We've come to retrieve it! It is our rightful inheritance as God's sons and daughters!"*

"Aaaaah, there it is!" she shot back at him. *"You have come to saaaave them, have youuuu?"* she mocked the man. Throwing her head back and

laughing at them all, convinced of her power, she snapped back and glared at the man until he shrunk back. *"Don't you mean, little one, that you have come to die?"* And with a talon disguised underneath the tresses of her dress, she reached out and grabbed him, easily tossing him into the river's torrent.

"Anyone else?" she laughed in cruel mockery.

In the next moment, Lord Jesus roared into the ranks, *"CHARGE HER!!!!"*

Responding like a flood, they swarmed her. Some jumped from the heights of the ravine, others ran carelessly down steep banks. All at once, she was surrounded and truly it was splendid to behold. All five armies worked as one, flying at her without fear. Lord Jesus flew above with His magnificent steed, and the realms of the angelic struck at her with all their force.

The five forces attacked her from every angle, pulling her down and deflating her falseness. All her finery and deception, even her grand tiara, were rent from her body. As if as a plague of giant locusts, swarming, bludgeoning and hammering, they beat her down and tore her limb from limb. Even what was left was annihilated by the warriors. And all those who'd fed off her ran like terrified imps into the forest surrounding them.

With her gone, the armies turned against the disgusting statue and decimated it as well, pulling apart all the evil it possessed.

Without someone to rule them, those in the river screamed out in fear. Believing the armies of King Jesus to be the enemy, they ran from them. The demonic rose in an attempt to protect their prey and fought the Lord's armies. All at once, the river was alive with dark activity as those who were held captive fought alongside their devilish captors, blinded by their familiarity. On and on, the battle continued for some time, as the armies of the Lord fought against the demonic horde.

All of the sudden, the prodigals pulled back and began to sing. Taking their wise lead, the four other groups fell into unexpected stillness and joined in their song. Beautifully they sang out over the lost of the murky waters.

Their simple song rang out with great power in the stillness:

Jesus loves me, this I know,
For the Bible tells me so.
Little ones to Him belong;

They are weak, but He is strong...

The result was instantaneous. Darkness froze as the lost stopped screaming and turned to listen. Over and over, they sang until deception's power melted like a hurricane backing out to sea. All hopelessness and rage dissipated under the power of their song until at last the lost received the invasion of Father's Love.

Sensing their moment had come, the last-days army, led by the prodigals, made a dash for the river. Swarming it, they grabbed hold of those caught in its grip and drug them from the murky water, all the while casting down the demonic declarations made over them. Furious demons grasped after them, but the Father's glory was invading even this dark place as love sang out.

Beloved, who had not lost sight of where her brother Daniel had been working, made her way to him now. He had been overcome by the sight of the false bride yet relieved by the arrival of the Lord's armies. Exhausted, he lay on his back near the river's edge, surrounded by those he'd saved from it. Still out of breath, he staggered to his feet as he saw Beloved running toward him and cried out, *"You've come, Beloved!"* His eyes closed in relief. Opening them again, he made sure she was really there. He cried out, *"Thank God you've come!"*

Throwing her arms around him, she set to work for his comfort, for she knew this great warrior must be tended to.

All around them was much activity as the river's population was drastically being depleted. The armies each found their inheritance and claimed it in their fashion. Disarmed by the familiarity of the prodigals and pressed by their desperate situation, the former prisoners were moved to trust those who'd come to save them and the murky waters were forced to relent its treasure.

As they invaded the realms of darkness, they retrieved countless souls once deemed as useless and hopeless as they themselves were once thought to be. They trampled the enemy underfoot, overwhelming him. He could give little defense.

The enemy of the Lamb bent in defeat, the work of his life stolen in a moment. The kingdom of darkness was raided and more hidden treasure was recovered and sent to the fields of grace...which were now heaven on Earth...the church, where newly trained treasure hunters awaited their arrival.

Having defeated their fallen foe, they stood and looked toward heaven. In unison, they cried, "FOR

THE KINGDOM OF HEAVEN AND THE LAMB
OF GOD!"

In Closing

SEVERAL MONTHS AFTER the great battle, Beloved was met by Lord Jesus. Excitedly, He took her hand and escorted her up the side of a rocky, mountainous path. Laughingly, He turned to her and said, *"Beloved, you need an ending."*

Reaching the top of a mountain she'd never seen before, Jesus happily explained that it was Mount Olivet. Sharing the joy of the surrounding landscape, He pointed out all the differing vegetation, rock formations and the beautiful olive trees. Taking the time to show her the different views He loved, He was quite familiar with every vantage point from that location and wanted to share every joyous memory with her.

After a beautiful time of rest and enjoyment together, Jesus turned to Beloved, hugged her tenderly and said, *"Dear one, this is where I left the earth and this is where I will return."*

He kissed her face and said goodbye, *"I will always be with you,"* and then He was gone.

Have You Read…

With the fate of the world in the balance, Beloved must rise above the deceptive snares of her adversaries to fulfill her calling: pursue the prophetic host and liberate the slumbering army of the Lord. Destined to wage war against the darkness, the army must be awakened to destroy the enemy's grasp on the world.

OTHER BOOKS BY VICTORIA BOYSON:

The Birth of Your Destiny: Just like a baby hidden in the womb, so are the promises God has given to us. He speaks to us of our future as if to conceive within us His will and purpose for our lives. Experience an impartation of God's grace and faith to fulfill all that God has for you through this powerful and insightful book.

His Passionate Pursuit: Victoria challenges you to embrace the captivating revelations of His passion for you— His beloved bride. It is an invitation to an awakening encounter with God. His Passionate Pursuit is a portal to heaven, unleashing God's presence into your life, empowering you with an impartation from His heart.

God's Magnum Opus: The Value of a Woman: God loved Adam so much, He created the greatest, most inspiring work of art He could for him—Eve! She was the expression of the Father's love. A priceless treasure, indeed! In woman, the Father created His Magnum Opus, His work of art—the grand finale of His creation masterpiece. In the Father's grand design for humanity, *you* are His magnum opus!

To contact the author or to order more copies of *Victorious: An Army Awakens*, please visit Victoria's website at www.VictoriaBoyson.com.

Victorious: An Army Awakens is available through Amazon.com, Christian bookstores and other online bookstores. It is also available as an eBook, purchasable through Amazon.com.

You can follow Victoria Boyson on Facebook, Twitter and Goodreads.

ABOUT THE AUTHOR

VICTORIA BOYSON is the founder of Victoria Boyson Ministries and Women of the Spirit Ministries, a ministry dedicated to raising up an army of women to impact and revolutionize their world. She is a passionate speaker, operating in extraordinary authority to awaken the church to their victorious reality. Through revelations of the Holy Spirit and the Word, Victoria is breaking down strongholds which have kept the church from fully realizing the great commission.

Based out of the Houston, Texas area, Victoria is called to awaken and prepare the bride of Christ for the end-time harvest and compel His church to embrace a passionate relationship with their heavenly Father. She is the author of *The Birth of Your Destiny*, *His Passionate Pursuit*, *Awakening: The Deep Sleep*, *Revolution: The White Horse Rider* and *God's Magnum Opus: The Value of a Woman*.